Their Night
to Remember

JUDY DUARTE

HARLEQUIN

SPECIAL
EDITION

HARLEQUIN®
SPECIAL EDITION™

Recycling programs
for this product may
not exist in your area.

ISBN-13: 978-1-335-40475-6

Their Night to Remember

Copyright © 2021 by Judy Duarte

This edition published by arrangement with Harlequin Books S.A.

For questions and comments about the quality of this book,
please contact us at CustomerService@Harlequin.com.

Harlequin Enterprises ULC
22 Adelaide St. West, 40th Floor
Toronto, Ontario M5H 4E3, Canada
www.Harlequin.com

Printed in U.S.A.

Since 2002, *USA TODAY* bestselling author **Judy Duarte** has written over forty books for Harlequin Special Edition, earned two RITA® Award nominations, won two Maggie Awards and received a National Readers' Choice Award. When she's not cooped up in her writing cave, she enjoys traveling with her husband and spending quality time with her grandchildren. You can learn more about Judy and her books on her website, judyduarte.com, or at Facebook.com/judyduartenovelist.

Visit the Author Profile page at Harlequin.com for more titles.

To Jeanne M. Dickson,
who has been one of my biggest supporters over the years, first by buying my books and then by reading the drafts of troublesome scenes. Jeanne is a talented author and offers a variety of suggestions that never fails to jump-start my creativity.

Prologue

Clay Hastings sat at the massive dark oak desk in his personal office at the family ranch, going over a legal brief. He was knee-deep into the document when the door creaked open and his father walked in without knocking, a crystal glass of his favorite bourbon in his hand.

In true Adam Hastings–style, he didn't apologize for the interruption. He merely launched into his reason for it. "You need to fly to Randolph, Colorado, tonight, Clayton. I told the pilot to file a flight plan and fuel the plane."

"What's up?"

"I just got off the phone with my private investigator. He told me Alana Perez is attending a cattle symposium there. I've approached her with several generous offers to buy her ranch, but she's turned her nose up at each one. And now she's not taking my calls."

Clay leaned back in his desk chair and crossed his arms. "Apparently, she doesn't want to sell."

"I get that. But the investigation revealed that the Lazy M is run-down and needs a lot of work. On top of that, this Perez woman doesn't know squat about ranching. It makes no sense for her to hold on to a property she can't afford. So I want you to meet with her in person and convince her that it would be in her best interest to sell."

Clay's father had built a cattle dynasty in Texas, which was impressive in its own right. But for some reason he'd yet to reveal, he was hell-bent on picking up multiple ranch properties near some out of the way town in Montana.

Most people who worked for Adam Hastings didn't question his orders, but then again, Clay wasn't like most people. And the youngest son of the Hastings family felt his differences every single time he talked to his father.

"What's so important about the Lazy M?" Clay asked.

"That particular ranch is the key to my new real estate venture. The state is very likely to build a new highway through that area. And if that happens, a couple more towns are bound to pop up and the land values are going to quadruple—at the very least."

So, that's what he had on his mind. "I take it the locals don't know about the highway."

"No." His father lifted his glass and swirled the bourbon, ice cubes clinking. "At this point, it's just a strong hunch on my part. So keep your mouth shut."

That made sense, but his father's plans often tended to straddle the line, and it was Clay's job as the family attorney to make sure his old man didn't take a step on the wrong side.

"All right, Dad. I'll go to Randolph. And I'll do what I can."

His father chuffed. "I'm not *asking* you to give it a try, Clayton. I'm telling you to *close* the deal."

Other than the *tick-tock-tick* of the clock hanging on the wall, the room went silent. Clay merely studied his father.

When Adam Hastings wore his gator-skin, custom-made Lucchese boots, like he did today, he stood nearly five foot nine. And thanks to a private gym on the ranch and a paleo diet, his weight never topped 156 pounds. Yet the cattle baron didn't need to be a big man to command—and demand—respect. Needless to say, when he gave an order, he expected it to be followed.

"The private investigator sent me Alana's picture. I'll send it to you along with the PI profile." His father took out his iPhone, pulled up a saved photo and sent it to Clay in a text. "She's a brunette, unattached and damn good-looking. Charm her. Do whatever it takes. Just convince her that it's in her best interest to take the money I'm offering her and buy a nice place in town, something she won't have to repair or renovate. I'll be doing her a favor."

Clay reached for his own cell, opened his father's text and studied the photo of a pretty woman in her late twenties or early thirties standing next to a dented old pickup, which was parked near a feed store. She wore a pair of faded jeans and a red plaid blouse. It was hard to tell how long her hair was. Long enough for her to pull it back in a messy ponytail. But there was no denying it. Alana Perez was attractive.

His father eased closer to the desk and placed his hand on the back of a tufted-leather chair, where he sometimes sat when discussing a lawsuit or a contract. He pointed to the brief. "What are you working on?"

"That countersuit against Ray Jennings and the Graham Group."

"That can wait." His father glanced at the clock on the wall, an antique that had been in the Hastings family for generations. "It's getting late. You've got a long drive back to Houston." Then he said, "I'll never understand why you refuse to move back home. There's more than enough room for you to live on the Double H."

True. His father had plenty of space for Clay in the sprawling ranch house, but he'd never been able to find much room for him in his heart. As a kid, rather a teenager, Clay once had tried to earn that kind of relationship with his father. It hadn't worked. But now he'd settle for his respect. If he pulled off closing this deal, his dad would be more than pleased. And deep down, Clay wanted nothing more than to oblige the father he'd hardly known until he'd turned thirteen, and he'd been trying to live up to his new surname ever since. And to prove he was more than a dirty little secret.

"I prefer living in the city," Clay said. But in all honesty, putting some distance between his family, his work and his personal life had been one of the smartest things he'd ever done.

"I still think it's foolish for you to waste the time and the gas on an unnecessary commute. You spend a lot of your free time out here anyway."

That's because, while Clay may have implied that he liked nights on the town, he'd much rather unwind on a Friday evening by riding Titan, the gelding he kept in the Double H stables.

But there was always a trade-off with his father, wasn't there? Life seemed to be one negotiation and compromise after another with the man that he never really felt like he understood. After all, he was the illegitimate son—the black sheep who'd been hidden from the rest of the family.

His father pointed to the legal brief resting on Clay's desk. "Put that countersuit on hold. I want you in Colorado tonight. So go home and pack."

Clay sucked in a deep breath and blew it out softly as he pushed aside the paperwork and got up from the desk. If truth be told, attending that symposium would be a lot more interesting than being cooped up in his office.

He gathered the papers on his desk and slipped them into the file. "Whatever you want."

"This land deal is very important to me," his father added. "And to this family. Just make it happen. I don't care how you do it. Hell, charm the pants off of her."

Clay's gut clenched. He'd never resort to that tactic. Using a woman—or anyone, for that matter—went against his moral code, which he must have inherited from his mother, since neither of his two half brothers would have balked at the assignment.

"I'll close the deal," Clay said. "But I won't resort to seduction."

"Dammit, Clayton. Don't get your hackles up. It's just a figure of speech. The last thing I want you to do is hop into bed with that woman."

That was the last thing Clay wanted, too.

Chapter One

Bent over the porcelain throne in the guest bathroom and holding her long black hair out of the way, Alana Perez lost her breakfast once again.

Callie, her best friend and roommate, stood beside her, a cool, wet cloth in her hand, securing her role as the best friend ever.

Puking her brains out was a pain, but Alana didn't mind the inconvenience. When she was twenty-two, she'd had a tubal pregnancy and an emergency surgery. Losing the baby she'd dearly wanted had broken her heart. But there'd been complications and an infection. And when the surgeon told her it was unlikely that she'd ever conceive again, she'd been crushed.

For the past ten years, she'd never had a reason to question that diagnosis, but during one romantic evening in Colorado, a handsome stranger named Clay had swept her off her feet and proven the doctor wrong.

As the dry heaves came to an end, Alana felt Callie's fingers splayed gently on her back.

"Are you okay now?"

Alana swiped the back of her hand across her mouth, then nodded and straightened. Her gaze sought Callie's. "This part of pregnancy really sucks. Tell me it'll be over soon."

"That's right." Callie wiped her brow with the soothing cloth. "Just a few more weeks. Then you can enjoy the second trimester."

"Believe it or not, I'm enjoying the first one." Alana flushed the toilet. "Well, not *this* part of it. But the doctor told me the baby looks good and the pregnancy appears to be normal. So I have no complaints."

"I'm happy for you," Callie said. "I know how badly you've wanted a baby and a family of your own."

After washing her face and hands at the sink and drying off, Alana followed Callie out of the bathroom and into the small, cozy living room with its scarred hardwood floor, dingy white walls that could use a coat of paint and rustic fireplace, the stones stained from smoke and soot, the mantel a rough-hewn beam.

"Your baby will never want for love and a happy home," Callie said, "like you and I did."

Alana smiled. "That's true. I just…" She sighed. "I wish I had some way to tell Clay about the baby. I don't expect anything from him, but he deserves to know that he's going to be a father. Unfortunately, that's out of the question."

"You can't remember his last name?" Callie asked.

"No, it never came up. And I was too dazzled by his smile, by the fact a gorgeous and apparently rich guy would want to buy *me* a drink in the hotel bar. I knew nothing could possibly come from that night. He's an attorney, and I barely finished high school." She sighed. "You should have seen the expensive clothes he wore—from his Stetson to his fancy boots. And I barely have a pot to pee in or a window to throw it out of. Besides, we live in different states, and I had a ranch to run. So I didn't want to jinx it."

From the moment he'd caught her eye, something wildly romantic had sparked between them, shooting off a flurry of pheromones to dance in the candlelight, sending her hormones spinning dangerously out of control.

She could blame it on the drinks, on the fact that he seemed to be nearly as mesmerized by her as she was by him, but she'd known exactly what she'd wanted and how she'd hoped the night would end.

And it had.

Now here she was, three months later—pregnant with a baby she'd never imagined possible.

She'd told herself that the memory of a magical night with a handsome stranger would be enough for her. But it hadn't been. She'd regretted her decision to slip out of his room the next morning without talking, without getting his last name—or giving him hers.

But she'd come away with more than a memory of that night; she'd been given a miracle to have and to hold.

"Where does Clay live?" Callie asked.

"I'm not sure." Alana plopped down on the faded tweed recliner that had been her grandfather's favorite chair. "All I know is that he lives someplace in Texas. He told me he was an attorney, but I don't know what his specialty is." Alana shot a glance at Callie. "I'd like to tell him about the baby, but I have no way of finding him."

"Hmm," Callie said. "Maybe we can come up with another way to find him. Did he mention which law firm he belonged to?"

Alana slowly shook her head. "Not that I remember anyway. I have to admit, I was a little dazed that night—and clearly running on hormones alone. So he might have said something, but if he did, it went *poof*."

Admittedly, she'd known leaving—not just his room but the hotel—and heading to the airport in the wee morning hours before he'd woken up had been stupid. But making love with him hadn't been a mistake. Their meeting had been predestined, it seemed. Because Alana was having a baby, a wonderful surprise—a gift—and she would finally have the biological family she'd always wanted.

Clay sat behind the wheel of the black Range Rover he'd rented at the airport in Kalispell and headed toward Fairborn. His GPS wasn't tracking the Lazy M—which he'd learned one fateful night in Colorado was also called Rancho Esperanza—so once he was in the general vicinity, he'd have to stop along the way and ask one of the locals for directions.

He should have made this trip to Montana three months ago, but he'd convinced himself that he'd done the right thing by waiting to contact Alana. And at the time, it probably had been the best move.

Having sex had been her idea, and she'd clearly meant it to be a one-night stand. That was all well and good, but Clay should have been a gentleman and suggested they wait until morning, when their heads were clear and he could reveal who he really was and his purpose for finding her. Unfortunately, several glasses of Patrón on the rocks had affected his better judgment.

And so had Alana, with her silky dark hair that sluiced over her shoulders, emerald green eyes with a fringe of black lashes and that pretty, waiflike smile. At that point, his moral compass had gone wonky, his libido had taken over and he would have followed her anywhere.

He could still see her lying on the bed, her face flushed with desire, her arms raised to him, inviting him to join her. Lust burned in her eyes, lighting him on fire. His hands explored each of her sexy curves. He'd never forget her sweet taste as his tongue sought hers or the sound of her soft mewls as she pressed her sex against his, rubbing. Needing.

Even if he'd wanted to forget about the woman who'd crossed his eyes and curled his toes, that scene continued to play on a continuous loop in his mind.

Damn. You'd have thought the memory would have paled by now, but it hadn't. Making love had been nothing short of amazing, and their chemistry had been off the charts.

Lulled by a soul-strumming afterglow, he'd fallen asleep while she cuddled beside him. Fully sated, he'd slept better than ever before. But when he'd woken up the next morning, the only thing he'd held in his arms was her pillow, where a hint of her floral scent lingered.

At the time, he'd had half a notion to fly to Montana and find her, but something had told him he'd better wait and give her a little time to put that evening behind her.

He'd hoped to do the same thing, but with each passing day, the memory of Alana had grown stronger.

And so had his guilt. He'd crossed a line that night by taking her to his room without telling her who he really was, and while he had a variety of reasons and excuses for doing so, none of them held water in the light of day.

As it was, once he'd returned from Colorado, and his father had questioned him about whether he'd been able to track down Alana, the owner of the Lazy M, he hadn't been entirely truthful. He'd said he had—but that she'd refused to talk to him once he'd mentioned his last name. The dishonesty grated on him, but he'd told himself that it wasn't an outright lie since that's probably how it would have played out anyway.

Of course, he knew that had been a self-serving crock of crap. But if his old man learned that he'd gone rogue—first in Colorado and now today— there'd be hell to pay.

And speaking of the here and now, Clay was finally going to see her again. He'd have his chance to lay his cards on the table and apologize for not speaking up sooner. He'd blame it on the alcohol-and-hormone-induced buzz. Then he'd negotiate a great deal, one that she'd appreciate after he put the right spin on it. Then he'd ask her out to dinner and take her on a real date, one that required a flight on the family jet to someplace fun and exciting.

A grin tugged at his lips—until his cell phone rang. The Darth Vader–themed ringtone turned his smile to a frown.

Clay swore under his breath. *What now, Dad?*

As the youngest of three sons—and the only one born on the wrong side of the sheets—Clay had always tried to earn his father's love, something he'd eventually given up on, but he still sought his old man's respect.

Unlike the other men in his family—good ol' Dad, a brother who spent most of his free time on the golf course or at a high-stakes poker table and another who juggled his lovers like Casanova on steroids—Clay had always been honest although, granted, that honesty had taken a recent fall from grace. But being completely truthful with his father was going to be tough when answering this incoming call.

In spite of the compulsion to let it roll over

to voice mail, he blew out a sigh, then using the display on the car's dash, pushed Accept. "Hey, Dad. What's up?"

"I expected to see you today. Where are you?"

Clay had learned to be creative when skirting a direct question. "Last night when I was leaving, I told Rosina to remind you that I'd be off-the-grid for a while."

"Yes, I know. But where the hell are you?"

Clay glanced out the windshield at the lush green scenery, at the snow-capped mountain peaks in the distance. "Don't you remember? I scheduled time off. I thought I'd do a little fishing." Not exactly a lie. He wasn't using a rod and reel, just his wits.

"When will you be back?"

"In a week."

His father let out a disgruntled sigh. "I need some real estate documents drawn up, and I didn't want Rosina to do it."

"What'd you buy?"

"Another ranch in Montana."

That was the best news Clay had heard in months. Ever since he'd met Alana and learned about her background—that she'd been raised in foster care and had finally met her only living relative, a dying rancher who'd made her his heir—he'd understood why she'd been so determined to hold on to the property. And for that reason, he'd been trying to steer his father in another direction. This new land purchase meant his efforts had worked. "I'm glad to hear it, Dad. Now you don't need the Perez property."

His father chuffed again. "The hell I don't. That new purchase won't do me much good unless I have that piece of land, too. And that woman's still not taking my calls."

She'd probably gotten tired of being harassed. When Clay's old man got a moneymaking project in mind, he zeroed in on it, full steam ahead.

"I don't mind you taking a week's vacation," his father added, "but once you've caught a few fish and are back on the grid, I want you to give me a call. You got that?"

Oh, he'd heard him, all right. For years, whenever Adam Hastings told Clay to jump, he always asked "How high?" In college, he'd even changed his major to please his father—albeit begrudgingly.

Anyone can run a cattle ranch. You're smart, kid. Smarter than your brothers.

I'm not cut out to work indoors, Dad. I actually enjoy ranching.

You don't need to waste your life dealing with a bunch of dumbass animals. I see you as my right-hand man—in all my dealings. Go to law school. I need an attorney I can trust.

Trust had been the magic word. So Clay had

given up his own plans for those of his father, a powerful man who'd been little more than a myth to Clay the first twelve years of his life and a conundrum ever since. So he'd done as he'd been told, passed the Texas state bar. Now here he was, five years later, still on his father's payroll—and still under his thumb, a position that was growing more and more uncomfortable with each passing assignment.

"Are you still there?" his father asked, pulling him out of his thoughts.

"Yeah, I'm here."

"You didn't respond. We must have a bad connection."

They'd never had a good one, although Clay had tried to do his part. Always reaching, always seeking to earn a place in a family that resented his sudden appearance in their lives. There were times when he suspected that resentment had never really gone away. But what the hell. He'd learned to live with it. He'd had to. Once his mom died, he'd had no other choice.

"Clayton?"

"Sorry. I'm driving. I just passed through a dead zone."

"I was talking to you about the Perez property, Clayton, and about you making it your highest priority."

It clearly was his father's. And now it was Clay's, too, for more reasons than one.

He slowly shook his head and bit back a sigh of frustration. "What makes the Lazy M so special? Why is it the key to this new real estate deal?"

"For now, all I can tell you is that it's strategically imperative we secure that land. When you get back, we'll discuss a new plan to get the ranch."

"Okay, Dad. But do me a favor. Let me have some time to relax. I'll work on it—you don't need to call every minute."

"I won't. But time is of the essence, Clayton. We've got until July to close the deal."

"And then what?"

"You'll see, but that Perez woman is going to wish she'd accepted any one of my generous offers."

Something about his old man's abrupt tone and the implication that he'd do something underhanded if he had to didn't sit well with Clay. And he'd have to act to circumvent his father's plans.

Maybe, once the surprise wore off and he had a chance to have a heart-to-heart business chat with Alana, he'd be able to either close the deal— or negotiate some kind of offer that might appease both parties.

But he'd need some time to do that. And one week might not be enough. "I'll tell you what, after my vacation, I'll stop off at the Lazy M and talk to her again."

"Don't just talk to her. Make her see reason." Then, on that note, his father ended the call without saying goodbye.

Clay's stomach knotted. What was his dad's plan B?

He continued down the two-lane country road to Fairborn. But his mind wasn't on the scenery. For the past three months, he'd been beating himself up for not setting things right with Alana. Or for not being completely honest with his dad. And it was high time he did both.

He'd make this right. He'd fix things. And he'd rely on his own plan.

He'd start by telling Alana his last name and admit his affiliation with Hastings Enterprises. Then he'd somehow convince her to sell the ranch and purchase something brand-spanking-new. If she furnished it with her grandfather's furniture, she could keep that family connection she so badly wanted.

He wasn't sure what she'd say when he showed up at her ranch today, but he'd already prepared his speech.

The way he saw it, he'd work out a win-win for everyone involved. Hastings Enterprises would get the property his father was gung ho on purchasing and Alana would get a beautiful new house in town, where she'd have access to grocery stores and shops and whatever things small-town folks did for fun.

And, if Clay played his cards right, and assuming Alana was willing, he'd get to spend another evening with her.

On the outskirts of Fairborn, Clay spotted a sign advertising the Tip Top Market and Casino, which was a mile ahead. That ought to be a good place to purchase a thirst-quenching drink and to ask one of the locals how to find the Lazy M since the address wasn't coming up on his GPS.

Moments later, he pulled into a graveled lot and parked next to a beat-up white pickup, the engine running, the radio blaring.

The driver wore a dusty, battered cowboy hat and sported a scraggly moustache. The sleeves of his red plaid shirt had been torn off at the shoulders, revealing a large, coiled rattlesnake tattoo on his left arm, which rested on the open window as his fingers tapped to the beat of the country tune.

Tattooed Cowboy cut a glance at Clay, then checked out the rented Range Rover. His bushy brow lifted, and the hint of a smile indicated his appreciation for the vehicle. No surprise there. It was an expensive set of wheels and only had about five hundred miles on it.

As Clay unbuckled his seat belt, he studied the small store. So *this* was the Tip Top Market and Casino? It looked like a case of false advertising to him. But what the hell.

After locking the Range Rover, he started toward the entrance to the market.

"Nice car you got there," Tattooed Cowboy said with a smile. "Must have cost you a pretty penny."

Normally, Clay would have ignored the comment and continued on his way, but there was no need to be rude to the locals, especially if he had his eye on the Lazy M.

"It's a rental," he said, as he continued to the front entrance.

He'd no more than reached for the door when it swung open and a heavyset guy wearing a red baseball cap and smelling of stale tobacco walked out with a case of beer in his arms. He nodded at Clay. "How's it goin'?"

"Not bad." Clay waited for him to pass, then entered the market, which seemed to carry the basics, including snacks and canned goods. But what really stood out was a pair of slot machines that sat to the right of the cash register.

An elderly woman wearing a floral-print blouse and pink slacks sat on a stool in front of one of them, her brown purse clutched tightly in her lap, a red walker adorned with a fluffy blue boa parked at her side.

This wasn't what Clay would call a casino, but then again, what did he expect? Fairborn was a far cry from Vegas. Apparently, the two slots served their purpose.

He stood just inside the door of the small store, noting a refrigerator case along the far wall. On top, a white sign with yellow edging had the word *Dairy* spelled out in blue swirly letters. He figured that's where they'd stock the cold drinks, too.

Before he took a step in that direction, a sixty-something blonde wearing a green shopkeeper's apron approached the register with a roll of receipt paper in her hand. When she spotted Clay, she brightened. "Hello, there. You must be new in town. I'll bet you're one of our new neighbors. We've had a couple of ranches sell lately."

"I'm just passing through," he said. "Nice town you have here, though."

"Fairborn is the best place in the world to live, if you ask me." She smiled, shifted the roll of paper into her free hand and reached out the right to give Clay's a shake. "My name's Carlene Tipton. Me and my husband Ralph own this place. We've lived in the area all our lives. We know just about everyone. So if you're interested in relocating, we know who's lookin' to sell." She laughed. "Heck. Me and Ralph might as well be Realtors."

Clay returned her smile. "I'll keep that in mind."

"Can I help you find anything?" Carlene asked.

"No, I've got it." He'd no more than taken a couple of steps toward the refrigerator section when a buzzer went off on one of the slot machines and red lights began to flash.

The elderly gambler threw up both arms, knocking her purse to the floor, and yelled, "Woo-hoo! Yahtzee! I win again!"

Carlene gave a little clap and called out, "Way to go, Betty Sue. You're the luckiest woman I know." Then she leaned toward Clay and lowered her voice. "That's my husband's aunt. She has a little dementia, so she lives with us. She's also got a little gambling problem. So we put the slot machines here in the store so we could control her spending. She's pretty much the only one who uses them. We've got 'em set up to randomly pay out a third of the time. It keeps us from having to file for bankruptcy. And, since Betty Sue hangs out at the store with me now, I can keep a good eye on her."

Clay chuckled. "That's smart."

Carlene puffed out her chest. "It was my idea. And I gotta tell you, it sure takes a lot of stress off me."

Clay walked over to the refrigerator case, retrieved a bottle of cold water and headed back toward the register. As he neared the slot machines, the woman, in her late seventies, stopped playing and gave him a once-over.

She'd tied a light blue scarf on her head to hold her curly red hair away from her craggy face.

He gave her a polite nod, prepared to go about his business, until she chuckled and offered him a bright-eyed smile. "Well, now. Aren't you a pleasant surprise? We don't see too many good-lookin' strangers around here, let alone city slickers."

Clay wasn't sure how to respond, but he sent her a charming smile. "What gave me away?"

"Them loafers. That fancy white shirt. The stain on your cuff looks like ink. No matter how you wash it, that ain't gonna come out." Her green eyes twinkled. "You got a name?"

He hadn't planned to introduce himself to anyone, but he supposed a woman who probably wouldn't remember him tomorrow didn't count. "My name's Clay. How 'bout you?"

"Betty Sue McInerny. Everyone around here calls me Aunt Betty." She sat upright, her brown purse still clasped tightly in her lap. "My nephew and his wife own this place. Where're you from, Clay?"

"Originally? California." Until his mom died. "But I live in Texas now."

"Auntie," the store owner called out as she swept in to rescue him from the chatty woman. "Please don't bother the customers."

Betty rolled her green eyes, mumbled something then went back to her gambling.

Clay and Carlene returned to the register, just as the tattooed cowboy entered the store.

"I'll be right with you," Carlene told him.

He nodded. "No rush, I just need a pack of smokes."

Carlene tapped her finger on the bottle of water Clay had placed on the counter. "Will that be all?"

"Yes, that's it. How much do I owe you?"

"A dollar forty-nine. I hope you have cash. We can't take credit cards today. Our server is down. And we don't take personal checks."

Clay reached into his rear pocket and pulled out his gold money clip, a gift from his father. *Money is power*, his old man had said when he gave it to him. *You can never have too much. Wear it with pride.* Actually, he'd felt a little awkward in accepting it—and more so when using it—but he hadn't wanted his dad to think he didn't appreciate the thought behind it.

After he peeled off a five, he waited for Carlene to make change.

"There you go," she said.

"I need directions to the Lazy M Ranch. I hear

it's called Rancho Esperanza now." Clay nodded toward the tattooed cowboy. "But why don't you help this fellow first."

"Thanks, man," Tats said to Clay before making his request to the store owner. "I'd like a pack of Lucky menthols, ma'am." He glanced at a display of lollipops. "And throw in a couple of those suckers."

Carlene turned, opened the locked case behind the register and removed the pack for the guy. Then she handed him the candy. As she rang him up, she continued to chat with Clay. "Jack McGee used to own that ranch. He died last winter." Carlene clicked her tongue. "Cancer. Tough break. Alana, his granddaughter, inherited his estate—if you can call it that. Needs a lot of work, though. But she's young. Anyway, it's about three miles to the south. The gates have been torn down for years, and even though you can see the driveway from the road, there's a bunch of weeds and shrubs that hide the entrance. But when you see a mailbox that's painted a pretty John Deere yellow and green, you'll need to turn to your right about a hundred yards down."

Tats picked up his cigarettes, pocketed his change and tipped his hat at Clay, then headed for the door.

"You got business at the ranch?" Carlene asked.

"No."

She nodded, as if he'd let her in on a big secret. "Just visiting friends, then. Alana and Callie
both live there, although last month, Callie married Ramon Cruz and moved to town. Ramon's
running for mayor. Election's right around the
corner, too."

Clay merely nodded at what seemed like unnecessary information—other than the fact that
Alana might be living alone, which would make
it easier for them to talk.

Carlene lowered her voice. "Callie's expecting
twins, and Alana is having a baby shower for her
at the ranch. I'm not sure if it's a surprise or not,
so please don't say anything."

"I wouldn't think of it," Clay said, hoping Carlene wouldn't snatch her phone and alert Alana
to his visit before he reached the ranch.

After thanking her, he left the store, eager to
be on his way. He climbed into the Range Rover
and started the engine. But he took a quick minute to check his messages. None so far. Good.

While following Carlene's directions, he kept
his eyes peeled for the green-and-yellow mailbox,
which ought to be coming up soon.

Up ahead, he spotted the old white pickup Tats
was driving. The hood was up. When Tats spotted Clay driving that way, he raised his arm to
flag him down.

Clay doubted many vehicles came along here,

so he pulled off to the side of the road and parked. He shut off the engine, got out of the Range Rover and walked past an oak tree and toward the truck.

"Car trouble?" he asked.

Footsteps sounded behind him, but before he could turn completely around, a shadowed figure rushed him, lifted what appeared to be a tire iron and slammed it against the side of his head.

Clay opened his mouth to yell, but no sound came out, and as he dropped to the dirt, everything faded to black.

Chapter Two

While the two ranch dogs sat beside Alana, watching her every move, she knelt in the garden she'd lovingly tended for the past few months. She'd enjoyed watching the plants sprout and the vegetables grow. Now she was reaping the first zucchini and cucumbers of the season. She might have inherited Grandpa Jack's cattle ranch, but she'd begun to think of herself as a natural-born farmer.

A smile tugged at her lips. Imagine that. For as long as she remembered, she'd worked to find her place in the world, but she'd never expected to find it just outside Fairborn, Montana.

She looked up from the wicker basket she'd filled with today's harvest and scanned the yard. It certainly looked a lot better than it had last year, when she'd first arrived to meet and then take care of her grandfather.

The once-dry grass had turned green, and the overgrown plants and bushes were trimmed. Even the old red barn, which still needed a new door and a fresh coat of paint, didn't look nearly as weathered and broken-down with the flowers in bloom along the sides of the structure.

She lifted her hand to shield her eyes from the late-afternoon sun and gazed at the orchard. All six of Grandpa's cherry trees looked strong and healthy these days. And after years of neglect, they'd begun to bear fruit. It was amazing what regular watering would do.

A little love and hard work had sparked new life into the old family homestead. And that, she decided, was a sign that her own life finally had purpose.

Alana remained kneeling, but she sat back, resting her derriere on her heels. She placed her hand on the beginning of a baby bump, still amazed at the miracle that grew there. For the past ten years, she'd been led to believe that she would never experience the joys of pregnancy, and now here she was, expecting a baby who'd be born during the holiday season. She'd have something to be truly thankful for this Thanksgiving and something to celebrate at Christmas.

Rascal, the black-and-white Queensland Heeler mix who'd once belonged to Grandpa, let out a yawn, then rested his chin on his paws. Next to him sat Chewie, the scraggly brown mutt she'd found wandering on the ranch a few months back and rescued. Chewie had been named after Chewbacca, the Star Wars character. There was a resemblance, she supposed. But Chewie could have just as easily been named Dust Mop. Either way, the scruffy dog was a real sweetheart. And so was Rascal.

The screen door squeaked open, and Alana turned to see Katie Johnson, the college student who, along with her much younger half brothers, had moved into Rancho Esperanza last month. Alana's longtime friend and roommate, Callie, had introduced Alana to the young woman who'd been working her butt off trying to care for the boys while taking a couple of classes at the junior college and holding down two part-time jobs. The poor girl had found it harder and harder to pay the rent.

Alana couldn't very well allow Katie to struggle in supporting her little brothers, especially when she and Callie were living in this big old house and had the old foreman's quarters available. So she'd opened her home and heart to the little family. One of the many reasons she wouldn't sell—no matter how many times land-grabber Adam Hastings called her with increasingly insistent offers.

"Alana," Katie called out before walking onto the porch with a glass of ice tea. "It's time for a break."

"Yes, it is."

Katie crossed the yard, walked to the garden and handed the glass to Alana.

"Thanks for the reminder," Alana said, taking the refreshing drink. "I was getting thirsty."

Katie folded her arms across her chest like a mother scolding a child. "You shouldn't be working so hard in your condition."

Now that she'd reached her second trimester, she'd let Katie and her brothers in on her condition. "Being in the garden doesn't feel like work." Alana took a refreshing drink, then lowered the glass and smiled. "It's actually very peaceful out here."

Chewie lifted her furry head and woofed, her bushy tail sweeping back and forth, stirring the dirt. Just like everyone else who lived at Rancho Esperanza, the stray had settled in and found a new home. The sweet little dog was especially fond of Katie, who loved animals and hoped to become a vet.

When Katie stooped to give Chewie an affectionate pat, the shaggy-haired pooch rolled over, providing access to her belly, which had filled out now that she was eating regularly.

"You know what?" Katie said, as she straightened. "I think Chewie's pregnant."

Alana glanced at the cattle dog, who lay nearby, his head resting on his paws, and smiled. "Apparently, his name suits him. He really is a rascal, isn't he?"

Rascal's ears perked up, and he turned his head. Then he jumped up and ran toward the driveway with Chewie on his tail, both dogs barking up a storm.

Alana didn't give them too much mind until Katie gasped, pointed and cried out, "Oh, my gosh. Look!"

At that, Alana turned and spotted a man staggering toward them, his face covered in blood. She hesitated briefly, her hand instinctively reaching for her growing tummy. When the stranger swayed and stumbled, she realized he was clearly hurt and not a threat to her or anyone else. So she set the glass of ice tea on the ground beside her, scrambled to her feet and, without taking time to brush the dirt from her denim-clad knees, rushed toward the injured man, ready to offer assistance.

"I'll get the first aid supplies," Katie said, as she took off in the opposite direction.

The dogs continued to bark at the man as he approached the house. He stood about six feet tall, or would if his shoulders weren't slumped, his head bent.

Had he been in a car accident?

Alana reached him just as he dropped to his knees with a thud, his body swaying to remain balanced.

"Oh, God." What should she do? How could she help?

When she reached the spot where he knelt, the dogs circled him, barking out a warning. She shushed them. "I've got this, you guys. Go back to the house." As the dogs obeyed, Alana squatted beside the man. "Mister? Can you hear me?"

He mumbled incoherently.

This was bad. *He* was bad. And he clearly needed a doctor. Only problem was the nearest hospital was twenty miles from here.

The front screen door opened, then slammed shut as Katie hurried toward them with a wet cloth and the first aid kit. "Here you go."

Alana took the cloth, but she wasn't sure where to start. Blood from an obvious head wound covered his face and had dried in his sandy-blond hair. She began to wipe his brow. He flinched but didn't move from the place where they both knelt.

"He's going to need an ambulance," Katie said. "That first aid kit isn't going to cut it."

"I know." Alana blew out a sigh. "But it'll take them at least thirty minutes to get here, if not longer. It might be better if I drive him straight to the hospital."

Katie seemed to think about that for a moment. "You're probably right. But maybe it's not as bad as it looks. Head wounds bleed a lot, even when they're relatively minor. I'll get a bowl of warm water and more cloths." Then she hurried back to the house.

As Alana carefully dabbed at the man's face, he winced and mumbled to himself. It broke her heart to see him in such pain.

"It's okay," she said softly, gently pressing the wet towel near his swollen eye. "I'm going to take care of you."

He seemed to believe her, and as she continued to wipe the blood from his face, he appeared slightly familiar. Had she seen him before? Maybe he was one of her neighbors.

His clothing, though, while torn and dirty, looked as if it might have been expensive, certainly before his accident. Which pretty much ruled out the Fairborn residents she'd met.

When Katie returned with a bowl of warm water and more cloths, she knelt next to Alana. "How bad is he?"

Alana used the replenished supplies and continued to clean his face. "The blood seems to be coming from a single gash on his forehead."

His eyes opened. Well, at least the one that wasn't swollen shut did. It was a pretty bluish-green shade. She'd seen a color like it before and—

Oh, no. It couldn't be.

But...

...it was.

Clay.

Alana's world tilted on its axis.

He closed his eye, then ran his tongue across parched lips littered with specks of dirt and dried blood.

"Clay?" Her voice came out in a soft whisper, although it was loud enough for him to hear her.

He merely looked at her. Blankly. "Huh?"

"Do you know who I am?" she asked.

He began to shake his head no, then grimaced in pain.

Dang. That accident had knocked him silly.

"Katie," Alana said, "would you please bring me the glass of tea I was drinking?"

"Sure."

Once Katie returned with the tea, Alana offered it to Clay, and he took a couple of sips.

Why was he here? And more confusing, how had he found her? She hadn't told him her name—or where she lived. And what in heaven's name had happened to him?

A flurry of other questions swept through her mind, but as his eyes shut and his body swayed, she realized he wasn't in any condition to answer them.

Alana turned to Katie. "Help me get him to the pickup. I've got to take him to the ER."

"Okay. But it's not going to be easy. And he won't be much help."

"I know. I'll bring the truck here. Keep an eye on him while I get the keys."

Moments later, her mind still whirling, she brought the pickup next to where Clay knelt in the dirt. She opened the passenger door, but as he struggled to stand then went down again, she realized Katie had been right. He wasn't going to be much help.

"I'm pretty strong," Katie said, "but I can't do it alone. And you really shouldn't be lifting him in your condition."

Maybe not. But Clay had been instrumental in putting Alana in her present "condition," and she owed him for that.

Besides, she'd run out on him once. There's no way she'd bail on him now.

By the time Alana reached the hospital in Kalispell, Clay had come to, although he still seemed pretty out of it.

"What happened to you?" she asked. "How did you get hurt?"

When he didn't respond, she cut a glance to the passenger seat where he sat, battered and looking completely clueless.

She suspected he'd been in a car accident, although she hadn't noticed a crumpled or disabled vehicle along the road, no broken glass, no indication of a crash. Her ranch was so remote, he wouldn't have been walking. And it wasn't likely that he would have been able to stagger too far on his own.

"Where…?" He glanced out the side window at the passing scenery, then turned to her with a furrowed brow. "Where am I?"

"Just outside of Kalispell. You're hurt, and I'm taking you to the hospital."

At that, he nodded, blew out a sigh and leaned against the headrest. They continued for a couple of miles in silence, then he shifted to study her.

She offered him a smile, hoping a friendly face would chase away his worry and confusion.

Apparently, her ploy wasn't working, because his brow furrowed deeper. "Do I know you?"

Her breath hitched and her stomach clenched. "You don't remember me?" she asked.

"Ma'am, I'm sorry. But right now, all I know is that I hurt like hell."

She wasn't a doctor, but her guess was that

his head injury had caused temporary amnesia. At least she hoped it would be only temporary. Surely, once he was on the mend, his mind would clear and his memory would return.

Then again, she'd just been a one-night stand. Amnesia or not, maybe he'd forgotten her, for real. But if that was the case, what was he doing here?

OMG. Had he come looking for her to say he had some kind of STD?

No, that couldn't be it. Her obstetrician had drawn blood and tested her for all kinds of things. Something like that would have turned up, and she was healthy. So was the baby. She blew out a weary sigh.

"What's your name?" she asked.

"I…" He gave a shrug and sighed. "I'm sure I have one, but I can't tell you what it is."

"Is it Clay?" she asked, hoping to give his memory a little nudge.

He gave a slight shrug. "That doesn't ring a bell."

What if his name *wasn't* Clay? What if he'd only told her that in Colorado? A lot of people used an alias when they met a stranger in a bar.

Or what if his memory never returned?

Clay moaned, closed his eyes and scrunched his brow.

This was bad. Really bad. The sooner she

got him to the hospital, the better. She accelerated until the speedometer topped eighty. All the while, she kept her eye on the road and a tight grip on the steering wheel. She might have the truck under control, but she didn't have any kind of handle on Clay's medical emergency.

When she spotted Green Valley General up ahead, she muttered, "Thank goodness," and turned into the driveway.

"Hang on. We're almost there." She followed the signs directing her to the emergency department and pulled right up to the front door, where a sign announced No Parking. Loading and Unloading Patients Only.

She honked her horn twice and was about to do it again when a rather burly-looking security guard wearing a blue uniform came to the automatic glass door. As he stepped outside, she reached for the control button on the driver's door and lowered Clay's window. "I need help. This guy is in bad shape and isn't able to walk."

The guard went back inside, and moments later, an orderly in navy blue scrubs hurried out the door with a wheelchair. And just as he'd probably done a hundred times before, he quickly and competently transferred Clay from the vehicle to the chair. Then he pushed him inside.

Alana wanted nothing more than to follow them into the hospital, to offer whatever help or information she could, which wouldn't be much. But she had to move the truck and let the medical staff do their jobs.

Five minutes later, after finally finding a parking spot in the busy lot, she made her way to the entrance where she'd left Clay in the hands of the orderly. The waiting room was packed. She scanned a sea of blurred faces, hoping Clay hadn't been left out here to fend for himself.

When the security guard spotted her, he took her to the door that led to the exam rooms. He punched in a code, then let her inside.

She wandered past several exam areas separated by pale green-and-white-striped curtains until a nurse wearing blue scrubs and carrying a file saw her.

"Are you looking for someone?" the nurse asked.

"Yes. My...friend is here. He has a head injury and is pretty banged up. An orderly helped him into a wheelchair and brought him inside."

"Oh, yes," she said. "Our John Doe. He doesn't remember his name. And when we checked his pockets, we couldn't find any identification. So I'm glad you're here. We have a few questions to ask you."

Too bad Alana didn't have many answers for them. The only thing she could honestly say is that his name could be Clay, that he might or might not be an attorney and that he possibly lived in Texas. The only fact she could be certain of was that he was a damn good lover—but that question wasn't likely to come up.

She followed the bustling nurse toward the back of the department. The doctors were going to want to know Clay's medical history, things that Alana, as the mother of his baby, would like to know, too. But they'd be on their own when it came to getting information.

The nurse stopped and pulled back the curtain, revealing the bed where Clay lay, as well as the blonde female doctor who was examining him.

"The patient's friend is here," the nurse told the doctor.

Alana was going to feel pretty stupid if she claimed to be a good friend, and then the man she knew as Clay turned out to be Joe Schmoe from Kokomo. But if she admitted that she didn't know much about him, they'd shoo her out of the room, and there was no way she'd leave. Not until she knew exactly who he was. And why he'd turned up at her ranch.

The doctor looked up, her green eyes zeroing in on Alana. "I'm glad you're here. What happened to him?"

"I'm not sure. I think he was coming to visit me, but instead of driving, he staggered onto my property. And when I asked him what happened, he couldn't tell me."

"We're going to run some tests," the doctor said. "He definitely has a concussion, but I can't rule out a skull fracture. He's somewhat lucid, but he can't provide us with any pertinent information. It looks like he has a case of amnesia. Hopefully, just temporary."

"He might've been involved in a car accident," Alana said.

The doctor shook her head. "No, it was probably a mugging. Or a carjacking. He doesn't have a wallet, cash, credit cards or any other form of identification."

Alana's breath hitched, and her heart cramped at the thought of something so mean, so brutal happening to Clay in her community. Someone had hurt him and could have killed him, then they'd robbed him and left him for dead.

"So what's his name?" the doctor asked.

Alana started to say Clay, then reeled it back in. They'd expect a last name, and she didn't have one. So John Doe might be more accurate. She paused for a moment, weighing what to do. Tell them the truth?

And then what? As a near stranger, she certainly wouldn't be privy to any updates to his medical condition.

It probably wasn't wise to give him a fake

identity, albeit one as temporary as his amnesia, but there was no way Alana was going to let anyone chase her off as a nobody. She needed information about her baby's daddy.

Then an idea popped up. A way to keep her story straight, to remember the details. "His name is Jack McGee. But he's kind of a drifter. I hired him to work on my ranch for the season."

The doctor nodded. "I see. Someone from the administration department will be up to get more information."

Alana could handle that. She'd provide them with Grandpa Jack's birthday, using her own birth year. And she'd give them the address for Rancho Esperanza. Hopefully, as soon as Clay's memory returned, the two of them would be able to straighten out this mess.

"Is Jack going to be all right?" she asked the doctor.

"I think so. I'm going to order a CT scan and some other tests. I'd also like to keep him overnight for observation."

Alana wasn't going to leave him here, completely defenseless. "Would it be possible for me to stay with him?"

"Sure, if he doesn't mind."

Alana glanced at Clay, who'd dozed off. "I'm sure he'll be fine with that."

Yet that was the second lie she'd told. She

wasn't the least bit sure how he'd feel about her camping out all night with him at the hospital or what he'd say if he were lucid. But she'd been given a second chance. And this was one night she wasn't going to slip out early, not without learning who he really was.

Jack woke up in a hospital bed, the morning sun lighting the room, if not his memory.

Wait. *Jack?* That couldn't be right. Could it?

For some reason, the name didn't seem to fit. But then again, nothing had been the least bit familiar to him over the past twenty-four hours. And on top of that, each nurse who'd come into his room, which had seemed like every fifteen minutes last night, had called him Jack. So he couldn't very well object. On what grounds?

He'd suffered an injury. That was for sure. But he'd be damned if he knew how it had happened. And no one else seemed to have a clue, either.

At least he was feeling a little better than he had yesterday, although his head still ached as if he'd been a piñata at a kid's birthday party.

He was also exhausted. Why did hospitals wake up sick and injured people when they needed their sleep?

And speaking of sleep, he turned to the right, where the brunette dozed in a chair by his bed. She'd been there all night. He'd seen her there each time he'd woken up. But he doubted she'd slept any better than he had. How could she?

She was pretty. That is, if he closed his bad eye and looked at her with only the good one. She was friendly, too. And she had a sweet, gentle voice.

Can I get you some water?

Are you cold? I can ask them to bring you another blanket.

Do you need something for pain?

Alana. The name sounded vaguely familiar. And she claimed that they were friends. But damn, wouldn't he remember a kind, thoughtful, stunning woman who looked like her?

But he clearly couldn't rely on that assumption. Hell, he didn't remember squat.

They *must* be friends, though. Why else would she be here? Not only that, she'd spent the night in a chair, which must be uncomfortable.

Another nurse—no, it was a doctor—walked into the room. Was she the same one who'd examined him last night? The one who'd run so many tests? Dr. Kirk…something?

"Good morning," the doctor said, approaching the bed. "I see you're awake."

At the sound of voices, Alana lifted her head and let out a little yawn.

"From the test results," the doctor continued, "your injuries aren't nearly as serious as they might have been. As I indicated yesterday, you don't have a skull fracture. Just a bad concussion. The night nurse said you did well, so I'm going to discharge you." Her focus shifted to Alana. "That is, if he has a place to go. And someone to look after him for the next couple of days."

"He can come home with me," Alana said. Then she cast her gaze on him. "That is, if you're okay with that."

He'd have to be. Where else would he go? So he nodded. But that didn't solve his problem. This whole damn situation left him flat-out bewildered.

"Give me some time to get the paperwork in order," Dr. Kirkland said. "I'll also give you instructions for follow-up care."

Alana rose from her chair. "Thank you."

As the doctor turned to leave, Jack came to his senses and called her back. "Wait a minute, Doc. I've got a few questions you haven't answered. Is my memory going to come back? And if so, when?"

"It should. With time." Dr. Kirkland slipped her hands into the pockets of her white lab coat. "But it's probably best if you get your rest and take it easy." Then she turned to Alana. "I'd suggest that you give him the time he needs to heal. Don't try to force him to remember."

Alana nodded. "Okay. Got it."

Jack certainly hoped she had a handle on things. Because right now, he couldn't seem to wrap his mind around anything.

Chapter Three

As the rickety old ranch pickup rumbled down the county road, engine rattling, seats bouncing, a country song playing on the radio, Jack remained silent. In fact, he hadn't uttered a sound since they'd left the hospital.

As much as Alana would like to start a conversation—she certainly had quite a bit to say to him—she was at a loss for words. Besides, the doctor said that, when it came to his temporary amnesia, they should let nature run its course.

She stole a casual glance across the seat at her injured passenger, a man dependent upon her for the time being. In spite of a few remaining flecks of dirt and dried blood in his sandy-blond hair, the stitches over his left brow and a bruised and swollen eye, she still found him drop-dead gorgeous.

He turned and caught her looking at him. As their gazes momentarily locked, her breath caught, and her grip on the steering wheel tightened.

"So what do you know about me?" he asked.

"Truthfully? Not much. Only what you told me." And she wasn't sure if any of it was true. "We really haven't known each other very long." Alana had a heart for people down on their luck, and her baby daddy had certainly hit a rough patch of it, but she didn't want to be naive anymore.

Her friend Callie had been pressing that reminder into her lately. People weren't always honest, and some would jump at the chance to take advantage of Alana's kindness and generosity. More than once, Callie had wagged her finger and said, *And just because they have money or appear to, that doesn't make them any more trustworthy.*

Her baby daddy cleared his throat, drawing her from her musing, and asked, "How did we meet?"

This was *so* not the conversation she wanted to have. Not here, not now. "I'm not supposed to overload you with information. Remember? It might work against you." And it could work against her. She wasn't about to tell him that he'd fathered her baby.

What if he wouldn't make a good daddy? What if he turned out to be the kind of man she didn't want to be a part of her child's life?

He let out a heavy sigh. "Look, I'm not asking you to provide me with a birth date, social security number or a mailing address."

If he were, he was out of luck.

During her days as a nanny, she'd learned it was best to answer a child's question simply and not to provide an explanation that was more than he or she could handle. And she suspected that same philosophy would work in this case. "We met in a bar."

He nodded as if that made perfect sense. Maybe for him but not for her. She'd never been one to hang out in places like that, let alone pick up a lover in one.

"Was it a bar around here?" he asked.

"No, it was in Colorado."

"What were we doing there?"

"I was attending a cattle symposium. And you didn't say."

He seemed to chew on that for a while, then asked, "When was that?"

"Close to four months ago." Dang. He was making it hard for her to follow the doctor's orders. And harder to hold off on having this particular conversation until he was well and able to remember that night. "I wish I could tell you more, but I can't. We'd both had a little too much to drink, and believe it or not, I barely remember more than you do."

When he turned his head and gazed out the side window, she assumed that she'd told him enough to appease him. So she continued to drive, her eyes on the road, then turned up the radio to let him know she was done talking.

She didn't blame him for wanting to know more about himself. But she had a few questions of her own that she'd love to have the answers to. The biggest one of all was *What the heck happened to you?* Yet plenty of others came to mind.

What were you doing in Fairborn yesterday? And why were you so close to my ranch?

Hopefully, with time, they would both get some answers.

He reached over and turned the radio knob, shutting off the music. "At the hospital, you told the doctor we were friends."

Only because they would have thrown her out of his room and not revealed any information to her if they'd been strangers. They might have been onetime lovers, and now they would be parents, but calling them *friends* was a pretty big stretch. "I don't want to throw too much at you until you have time to heal. Remember what the doctor said."

He chuffed. "Hell, I can't even remember my name. And even though you told me it's Jack, that doesn't seem right."

Would he feel any better if she'd called him Clay? She tightened her grip on the steering wheel, then her right hand slipped to her lap, gently caressing the curve of her belly. He'd seemed honest that night, but for all she knew, he could have been lying through his teeth, just to get her into bed.

Then again, going to his hotel room had been her idea, and she rolled her eyes at the thought.

In fact, they'd spent only one evening together, one unforgettable night. At least she'd never forget it. And even if that were possible, she'd have a constant reminder in about five months.

It seemed reasonable to suspect that, if he'd come looking for her, it meant he'd remembered it, too. That is, until someone or something knocked the sweet memory from his mind.

She pressed on the accelerator, pushing the beat-up old truck to drive faster. The sooner they got to the ranch, the more distractions he would have. And then maybe he'd stop asking the question she either couldn't—or didn't want to—answer.

They'd hardly gone another mile when he spoke again. "Have we…? I mean, did we…?"

...*have sex?* Her breath caught, and her heart

nearly skyrocketed out of her chest. *Yes. And it was…awesome.* The best she'd ever had. But surely that was too much to admit to now. Still, she couldn't very well ignore the question.

"Did we…what?" she asked, her voice coming out a little wobbly. "I'm not sure I know what you mean."

"Keep in touch. I assume we did. Do we see each other very often?"

Relief rushed through her, and she thanked her lucky stars he hadn't made the jump she'd thought he'd made. "Four months ago, we met and…enjoyed each other's company. I told you that if you were ever in the area, you should stop by the ranch. Apparently, before you got hurt yesterday, you planned to surprise me. So I figure that makes us friends. And I'm okay with that."

Was she? *Truthfully?* Yes and no.

She cut another glance across the seat, only to find him staring at her. And then he nodded, as if it all made sense to him.

Thank goodness. She started to blow out a little sigh, then sucked it back in as her relief faded.

Returning to the ranch wasn't going to solve her problems. Because something told her that her problems had just begun.

The old rattletrap pickup slowed next to an overgrown bunch of weeds and shrubs that nearly swallowed up a bright yellow-and-green mailbox. The right front wheel hit a rut of some kind, and the jarring awakened the dull ache in Jack's head.

"Here we are," Alana said, as she turned on the right blinker and continued past a broken wooden structure that had been a gate at one time.

So much for having a sense of privacy or keeping people off the property.

Alana had told the doctor that she'd found him on her place, but if this was where he'd collapsed yesterday, it didn't look the least bit familiar. But then again, nothing seemed familiar to him, not even Alana, who'd spent the night sleeping in a chair next to his hospital bed, which suggested that they might be more than friends.

"Have I been here before?" he asked. "I mean, before yesterday?"

"No," she said. "That was the first time."

Then, they weren't lovers? That didn't make sense, even to a man whose brain was a scrambled mess. Because what, other than sexual attraction, would provoke a man to come looking for a beautiful woman he'd met four months ago in an out-of-state bar?

He stole another look her way, this time his focus on the ring finger of her left hand, which rested on the top of the steering wheel. Nothing there. No tan line. No reason to believe she was married or engaged.

Not that he was in any position to let his mind, as jumbled as it was, wander in a romantic or sexual direction. Still, she'd spent the night next to his hospital bed, sleeping nearly upright. Why would a woman do something like that?

His gaze lifted to her face, to her delicate profile, to the thick black lashes framing big green eyes a man could get lost in if he wasn't careful. He couldn't help noting the way the sunlight glistened on the glossy strands of long dark hair. Rather than let her catch him looking at her again, he turned away. Instead, as they bumped along the rutted, potholed road, he studied her property, the expanse of pasture that hadn't seen any cattle, let alone a mower or plow, in years.

Deferred maintenance on a colossal level.

"So, this is your ranch," he said.

A broad smile dimpled her cheeks. "Yes, it is. People in town still refer to it as the Lazy M, but I call it Rancho Esperanza."

Hope Ranch? Jack didn't see much about this particular plot of land that would provoke hope. But the fact that he understood those two Spanish words was an interesting awareness. Was he fluent? He tried to summon up more words, but his head began to spin. Maybe later.

"I know it doesn't look all that great now,"

Alana added, "but it will be one day. Besides, we love living out here."

We? Did she have a family? Kids? A significant other?

"Who's 'we'?" he asked.

"Me and a few of my friends."

As the pickup pulled into the yard, he saw one of those friends, an attractive blonde, sitting in a rocking chair on the front porch. She got to her feet before Alana could shut off the ignition and started toward them. Actually, waddled was more like it. The woman was clearly pregnant and looked like she was ready to deliver any day.

"That's my friend Callie," Alana said. "She used to live here, but she moved out right after she married Ramon Cruz, our future mayor. That is, if the upcoming election turns out the way everyone seems to think it will. We're having a baby shower for her next Saturday afternoon."

By the size of her baby bump, she looked like she might give birth before then. But what did he know about pregnant women?

At least, he assumed he didn't know anything. He closed his eyes for a moment, trying to focus on women and babies, hoping things would come together for him, but they didn't.

Nope. He felt pretty confident that Jack didn't know jack about pregnancy or childbirth.

Alana shut off the engine, and they both climbed from the pickup.

"Hey there!" The blonde brightened as she crossed the yard to greet them. "I'm Callie. You must be—"

"—Jack!" Alana grabbed his arm. "I'd like to introduce you to my best friend and former roommate, Callie."

An odd expression crossed the blonde's pretty face, one of confusion. Or maybe more like surprise. Her brow furrowed, then she turned to Alana. *"Jack?"*

"That's right. I met him a while back, and I'm afraid he doesn't remember anything about himself, even his name." Alana withdrew her hand from his arm and took a step closer to her friend.

"I…" Callie scanned Jack's length, then she returned her attention to Alana. "I didn't see that coming."

"I'll explain later. I'm sure he'd like to rest for a while. His pain meds make him sleepy."

He found their conversation a little odd, but what difference did that make? It's not like he had anything brilliant to add. Though he was wondering why they were talking about him like he wasn't there.

Instead, he scanned the yard. The barn needed a fresh coat of paint as well as a new roof. The yard was in better shape—the grass was freshly mowed, the garden weeded. Six cherry trees grew across the driveway. They looked a little scraggly, but they were producing fruit.

Alana referred to her place as a ranch, but it looked more like a farm to him. Supposedly, he'd been here yesterday, the day he'd somehow gotten banged up, but he couldn't remember anything prior to waking in a hospital bed, his head aching like hell. It was better now, but she'd been right about those pain meds. He was beginning to feel pretty drowsy.

"Jack," Alana said, as she again reached for his arm and drew him from his musing. "Let's go inside. I'll show you to your room."

He didn't object as she led him to the house. Right now, all he could think about was lying down, closing his eyes and trying to take a nap. Maybe when he woke up, he'd even find that the last twenty-four hours had just been a bad dream.

Alana hated to leave Callie standing in the yard and looking more than a little befuddled, but a secret or two was in jeopardy, and since spilling the beans right now was out of the question, she couldn't get Jack into the house fast enough.

Yesterday, while they were at the ER and waiting for Dr. Kirkland to come back and share the results of the MRI, Alana had texted Callie, letting her know that Clay had shown up on the ranch and that something awful had happened to him. And it was anyone's guess just what that something was.

Throughout the afternoon and evening, she'd continued to give Callie updates about the head injury that had left him with temporary amnesia. She'd even told her BFF that the doctor was admitting him for observation. She'd also sent a text about an hour ago to say he was being released and that she was taking him back to Rancho Esperanza until he recovered.

Unfortunately, she'd neglected to mention that, when asked his name, she'd lied.

Sure, at the time, she'd had reasons for doing that, but as the day wore on, she'd begun to question her judgment. And by the time they'd checked out and she'd accepted financial responsibility for his medical expenses, she'd realized she should have been honest from the get-go. But she had no idea how to backpedal now, especially when the poor guy was struggling to remember anything at all. The way she saw it, lies and apologies would only confuse him more.

And yes, on top of that, the truth would be a huge embarrassment for her to admit to, but she was in too deep now to avoid facing the eventual consequences of her mistake.

Just as the old saying went, she'd made her bed and would have to, um, yeah. Been there, done that, four months ago, too. And like before, she'd have to lie in this one, as well.

She led her onetime lover through the small living room and down the hall to the bedroom that had once belonged to the real Jack McGee. She entered first, but when she turned to point out the en suite bathroom to her guest, she realized he remained in the doorway, as if reluctant to enter.

"Is something wrong?" she asked. She'd assumed the man had money—and lots of it. Was the room not to his liking; had it not reached his personal standard?

"Whose room is this?" He leaned against the doorjamb and folded his arms across his chest.

"It used to belong to my late grandfather. Why?"

"Just wondering. I picked up the scent of Old Spice cologne and pipe tobacco." He straightened, uncrossed his arms and took a deep sniff. "Peppermint, too."

The younger Jack's brain might be scrambled, but the blow to his head certainly hadn't affected his sense of smell.

"That's what I like about this room," she said, as she scanned the scarred antique furniture, the red, brown and green patchwork quilt that covered the double bed, the colorful braided wool rug that protected the hardwood floor. "Every time I walk in, I think of him." And how sweet he'd been, how appreciative and…how very much she missed him.

"I'll be careful not to open any windows and air it out."

She smiled at his unexpected thoughtfulness. "It's okay if you do. I didn't plan to lock up the room and turn it into a memorial. I just haven't gotten around to moving his things out. There's so much more to do on the ranch that it hasn't been a priority."

He nodded, then said, "I'd be happy to help out while I'm here and take on a few chores."

"You don't have to do that."

"Yeah, I know." He eased into Grandpa Jack's bedroom. "Consider it my way of paying you back for room and board. I'll also reimburse you for my medical bills—once I remember where I bank and can access my account."

She appreciated the gesture and made a mental note of it on what Santa would call Jack's naughty-or-nice list.

"All right," she said, "but for now, you need to get your rest and take the time to heal." And maybe as his memory returned, he'd remember some of the things she'd never forget.

"Will do."

That was her cue to leave and give him some privacy.

"The bedding is clean," she said.

He nodded toward the doorway that led to the bathroom. "If you don't mind, I think I'll start with a shower."

"You'll find towels and washcloths in the cupboard under the sink. There's a razor, too. I'm not sure about a toothbrush, though."

"I've got the one they gave me at the hospital. I think that bag is still in the truck."

It was. "I'll get it for you."

He was going to need clean clothes, too. So she walked to the closet and pulled out a pair of faded jeans and a blue plaid shirt with a frayed collar. "I realize this probably isn't your style, and it might be a little small, but it's something to wear while I wash the clothes you're wearing." She nodded at the dresser. "You'll find underwear and socks in the top drawer. I know—" She caught herself before admitting that she knew he had a preference for boxer briefs—and expensive ones at that. "I mean, I *hope* that you'll make yourself at home."

"Thanks. I appreciate all you've done, all you're doing."

"It's not a problem. If you'll set your dirty clothes outside the bedroom door, I'll wash them for you. I'm pretty good at getting out stains." She'd had to be. Buying new clothes had been a luxury when she was young. And these days, it still was.

He studied her for a moment, his head tilted slightly to the side. "It seems…odd…that you're letting me stay here. I mean, if we only met once and we haven't seen each other in months."

"If you knew me better, you'd realize you're not the only one I let move in temporarily. At dinner, you'll meet Katie and her two younger brothers. They're living in one of the outbuildings, but we all eat together. I hope…"

"You hope what?"

"That you feel better when you wake up, that things begin to make sense."

"You and me both."

Their gazes locked, and as much as she wanted to leave him to shower and take a nap, she couldn't seem to move. At least, not in an attempt to put a little distance between them. And that wasn't a good idea. Not today.

He was the first to look away. He nodded toward the bathroom. "I'd better take that shower and see if I can get some rest. I didn't get much sleep last night."

"I didn't, either."

"Yeah. I know. But what I can't figure out is why you spent the night in my room."

"Because…" It was too hard to explain yet too hard not to. But he wasn't ready for a rundown of that night in Colorado. And quite frankly, she wasn't ready to provide it. "Well, let's just say that

I've been told I'm a sucker for a sob story, but I listen to my instincts. I prefer to think that I have a big heart. Maybe too big at times, but I just can't help feeling sorry for people who are down on their luck. I want to do what I can to help, however little that might be."

And with that, she made for the door. If she wasn't careful, her big ol' heart was going to get her into trouble.

Moments later, after leaving Jack to shower, she went to find Callie. But she didn't have to go far. Callie sat on the brown tweed sofa in the living room, waiting for her.

"I've got him settled in Grandpa's room," Alana said.

"Good." Callie lowered her voice to a whisper. "What's going on?"

"He had nowhere else to stay, so I brought him home."

"Yes, I can see that. And knowing you the way I do, I'm not at all surprised. But I thought you told me his name was Clay. Did he lie to you in Colorado?"

"He might have. I don't know. But…" Alana took a seat next to her friend and blew out a wobbly sigh. "Well, when the doctor asked me his name, I told him it was Jack."

"Jack? Like your grandpa?"

"Um, yeah."

Callie turned in her seat, facing Alana. "Why on earth did you do that?"

"At the time, I was desperate to explain the inexplicable. And it just sort of rolled out of my mouth. Looking back, I should have leveled with everyone involved, but nothing made sense yesterday."

"You're going to be sorry for that."

Alana leaned against the backrest and slunk in her seat. "I already am. But I have no idea how to turn things back to right, if you know what I mean."

Callie chuckled. "I gotta tell you, I have no idea what you were thinking—or how you're going to fix it, either."

Neither did Alana. And she had a feeling that "Jack" already suspected that they'd been lovers or that they'd at least wanted to be.

What would he say when…no, make that *if*… he found out she was pregnant? Because the jury was still out on whether she should admit that he was the father or keep that secret to herself.

Only trouble was, she couldn't hide her baby bump much longer. And when Jack's memory returned, he'd only have to do the math.

Chapter Four

Alana tried to wake Jack to tell him to come to dinner, but he merely rolled over and said, "Okay," then went back to sleep.

Neither of them had gotten much rest the night before.

By eight o'clock, she was exhausted and turned in earlier than usual. As she tiptoed down the hall, she paused in front of Jack's room and quietly opened the door to check on him. She wanted to make sure he was still breathing. But her own breathing stopped the moment she spotted him asleep in bed, bare chested. A large, muscular right leg had snuck out of the covers, suggesting that he was sleeping in the raw.

She'd forgotten how darn good-looking he was, how perfectly formed, how taut his belly. Those arms, the impressive biceps, had once wrapped around her, holding her close as his hands and fingers had worked their magic on her body...

Oh, for Pete's sake. Enough of that. They'd made love nearly four months ago, and it may as well have been four years. She hadn't known anything about the man then. And heck, he didn't even know himself right now.

She took a step back, her hand remaining on the doorknob. She'd come to check on him, not gaze at him like a lovesick puppy. Or to drool over him.

So get out of here. You've checked on him. He's fine.

That he was. His breathing was steady, his well-sculpted chest moving up and down.

She inhaled deeply, and while she could still make out Grandpa's faint but lingering pipe tobacco, she also caught the scent of soap. She took a moment to savor the alluring smell, then slowly stepped away from his room and closed the door. Jack would no doubt slumber like a baby tonight, but she'd be hard-pressed to keep her memories and yearnings at bay long enough to fall asleep.

And she was right. She tossed and turned like a dried-up tumbleweed in a Texas windstorm.

The next morning when she entered the kitchen to start breakfast, the aroma of fresh-brewed coffee greeted her. The room was empty, but the coffee maker was still turned on, the carafe nearly full.

Alana had always been an early riser, but Katie, her temporary roommate, must have beat her to the kitchen. At dinner last night, she'd mentioned she'd have to pull an all-nighter to study for a microbiology test. The young woman had suffered appendicitis during the spring semester and had had to file an incomplete. She was making up the class during the summer.

Katie must have fixed the coffee so she could drink a cup before leaving. That being the case, she'd better check on Katie's brothers and tell them it was time to wake up and get their chores done.

Alana crossed the kitchen, walked through the mudroom and out the back door. Then she stopped in her tracks. Katie's car was still parked near the barn, so she hadn't gone to school yet. But someone else was awake.

Jack stood near the broken-down corral, his back to her. He held a white mug in his hand, the steam curling up into the morning air. The two dogs, Rascal and Chewie, sat on their haunches beside him, clearly accepting him as a ranch fixture—if not a friend.

When Alana met him in Colorado, he'd claimed to be an attorney and said his name was Clay. He'd certainly looked the part in that hotel bar. But today, dressed in Grandpa Jack's clothing, he appeared to be a real live cowboy. So much so, in fact, that it gave her reason to question his story about being a lawyer.

Unable to help herself, she stepped off the back porch and went outside to join him. He must have heard her approach, because when she got about ten feet from him, he turned around and eyed her carefully. He wore a curious expression, one that seemed to question her.

Had his memories come back?

"How're you doing?" she asked.

"Okay." He lifted the mug in his hand. "I hope you don't mind that I put on a pot of coffee this morning."

"Not at all." She tucked a loose strand of hair behind her ear. "You must be hungry. I can make some hotcakes. Or maybe scrambled eggs."

"Whatever's easiest. I've never been a big breakfast eater." He paused, raised an eyebrow, then he chuffed. "How 'bout that? I've remembered something else that isn't very helpful."

"Something else?"

"Yeah. I speak a little Spanish, too. Like I said, when it comes to a solid memory, I wish I'd get a better clue about me. Like my name, where I live. That sort of thing." He lifted his mug, took a sip then held it up to her. "Apparently, I also like my coffee black."

"Then, the doctor was right." Guilt and worry rose up and began to taunt her, but she tamped them down and forced a smile. "With time, your memories will come back."

"One by one, I guess." He turned toward the corral and peered out into the distance. "So what'd your grandfather run? Cattle? Horses?"

"Both. Kind of. He mostly raised beef cattle, but he was an old rodeo cowboy. So he also bred and trained cutting horses on the side. There are still about a dozen cows grazing out in the south pasture, and there are two horses left. Bailey and Selena. Grandpa asked me to exercise them often."

"Do you? Ride them?"

"I wish I could." She shrugged a single shoulder. "I'm not very good at it, and I forgot how to saddle them. I'll probably have to sell them. Grandpa said they were 'damn good broodmares.'"

"I'll saddle them for you."

"You know how to do that?"

"Apparently." He scrunched his brow, then slowly shook his head. "Maybe in a couple of days, I'll give it a try."

So he was an attorney and a rancher? Was that

even possible? She'd like nothing more than to trust every little thing he'd told her when they'd met, although he really hadn't revealed very much. She'd carried most of the conversation. And then, once they'd gone to his hotel suite, neither of them had been in the mood for idle chitchat. Their bodies had done the talking.

"Would you mind if I took a look at Bailey and Selena?" he asked.

"Not at all. I'll take you to the barn after breakfast." Yet instead of turning and walking away, she continued to study him.

"Is something wrong?" he asked.

"No. Not at all." But that wasn't true. She hated to think that he might have lied to her back in Colorado, that he hadn't been truthful about his name or his occupation, especially since she'd been so open and honest with him.

At least she'd been honest back then. Who was the liar now? She'd had her reasons for not telling him more about the night they'd met, but why in the heck had she told him his name was Jack McGee?

She'd have to figure out a way to set the record straight, but she couldn't see how to do that without going into detail about that one-night stand. And she shouldn't broach the subject until he was feeling better and his memory returned. So it wouldn't do her any good to stew about it now.

"I'll have breakfast on the table in twenty minutes," she said. Then she turned and walked back to the house. But guilt continued to dog her.

Callie had been right. Alana had a big problem on her hands. And since she was determined to save face, she had no idea how she was going to fix it.

Jack watched Alana head inside, unable to keep his eyes off the alluring, gentle sway of her denim-clad hips, her shirt flowing over them, or the way her long dark hair tumbled around her shoulders and down her back. Yesterday, after he'd woken up in the hospital, he'd found her attractive. But this morning, after the pain meds had worn off and he'd gotten a good night's sleep, he realized she was downright beautiful.

Her slight Texas drawl settled on his ears like a serenade on a treasured, well-tuned guitar. She also had a simple, country girl demeanor that appealed to him, although he wasn't sure why. For some reason, he didn't think he'd been drawn to that kind of woman in the past, although he couldn't say why he'd made that jump.

Still, something was off about her, about him. About them. And he couldn't seem to put his finger on just what it was.

But hell. Nothing about the surreal quagmire he'd stumbled into felt right. And he couldn't help thinking that, as kind and sweet as Alana had been to him, she wasn't being completely forthcoming about how they'd met or who he was.

Did he have a sixth sense about stuff like that? Or was he just prone to skepticism?

Maybe, when his brain healed, he'd figure it out. That is, if there was something to figure out.

No sense worrying about it now. He turned around and focused on the pasture beyond the corral and wondered how much property Alana had. And how many cattle she could run. It was going to take a boatload of cash and hard work to get this place productive again. But from what he could see, there was a lot of potential.

It was odd how he knew that. He'd been wearing designer clothing when he'd gotten hurt. Both the slacks and the shirt had Armani labels. And he also had on Gucci loafers. Other than the expensive brand names, the clothing didn't seem familiar.

He glanced down at the faded jeans he wore today, at the borrowed flannel shirt, both of which felt more comfortable than what he'd changed out of after his shower last night. And that wasn't just because the fabric was soft and worn. Or because they were clean and smelled like laundry detergent. There was something about them that stirred something deeper than the kind of comfort that was only skin deep, which didn't compute. Because he knew something about property and ranching, and that was as clear to him as the stitches and the lump on his head.

So who was he?

Apparently he had money and could recognize the finer things in life. He spoke a little Spanish. And his name was Jack.

Jack Maguire, Alana had told the doctor. Or was it Jack McGee? Hell, he'd be damned if he knew. He'd been drifting in and out at the time. Still, the name Jack McWhatever didn't sound the least bit familiar at all. He'd have to take a second look at those hospital-discharge papers, although they might not offer him any answers.

He blew out a sigh. How much longer would the blasted amnesia last? He sure as hell hoped he wasn't stuck with it for the rest of his life.

And what about that life? Was someone missing him? Did he have a family? A wife and kids? Parents? Brothers or sisters?

No one came to mind.

He tried to conjure thoughts of Christmas, but that didn't help. Wait. What about Hanukkah?

But nope. Neither one triggered a solitary thought. Not a tree or a dreidel. Not even a big-ass turkey dinner on Thanksgiving.

Apparently, he didn't have any holiday memories, either. At least, none that came to mind now.

He chuffed, then turned and scanned the property again. So, Alana's grandfather ran cattle and raised cutting horses. He was actually looking forward to checking out the mares that were stabled in the barn, although he wasn't sure why.

Damn. He hated not knowing squat about himself. He chugged the last drop of his coffee, then headed to the house for another cup. And to quiz Alana once more. She had to know more than she'd told him. Because if they'd met in Colorado, like she'd said, they must have talked about something. Otherwise, why had he shown up here?

By the time Alana reached the kitchen, Katie and her brothers were dressed for the day—Katie in black jeans and a gray T-shirt, the boys in their Little League uniforms. They sat at the table drinking orange juice and eating cereal and peanut butter on toast.

"I'm sorry you had to fend for yourselves," Alana said. "I meant to fix hotcakes this morning."

"Don't apologize," Katie said. "If I didn't have class this morning, I would have gladly made breakfast for everyone. As it is, I'm running late because I need to drop the boys off at Coach Ramon's house first. They have a playoff game at eleven."

Eight-year-old Mark, his big brown eyes bright and hopeful, looked up from his frosted corn-flakes. "Are you gonna come watch us, Alana? Coach said I get to start today."

Alana tried to attend most of their games, but she'd have to miss this one. "I'm sorry, sweetie. I can't make it today." She planned to stick close to the ranch. Jack seemed to be feeling better, but she didn't want to leave him alone yet.

And speaking of Jack, she needed to fix him something hearty to eat. He'd missed dinner last night, so he had to be hungry.

The back door creaked open and boot steps sounded in the mudroom as Jack made his way to the kitchen. He stopped short when he spot-ted the boys and their older sister seated around the table.

"Jack, this is Katie," Alana said. "And these handsome young ballplayers are her brothers, Jesse and Mark."

He gave a polite nod. "Nice to meet you."

Jesse, the youngest boy by eighteen months, stared at Jack, clearly examining his head injury— the stitches, the swollen brow, the bruising under his eye. "What happened to you?"

"Dude." Mark jabbed an elbow at his little brother. "Don't be rude."

Jesse frowned at the admonition. "I'm sorry,

mister. It's just that I had a black eye once. When I almost got hit by a car."

"You fell in the street," the eight-year-old corrected.

"Yeah, but it could have been really bad if the man hadn't stopped in time. I still banged my head super hard and got to ride in an ambulance." Jesse gazed at Jack. "Did you have to go to the hospital?"

Jack nodded. "Yeah. I did."

"Jess," Katie said, "stop asking so many questions. Jack probably can't answer them anyway. He doesn't remember what happened to him."

"I can't blame the kid for being curious," Jack said. "For all I know, I was kidnapped by aliens and then pushed out of their spaceship."

That brought on a couple of chuckles, lightening the mood around the table.

So Jack had a sense of humor. And he knew how to diffuse an awkward moment. Good to know.

"Boys," Katie said, "we have to get out of here. Finish your breakfast, then go get your gear and meet me in the car."

"Okay." Mark lifted his glass of juice and drained it.

Jesse bit down on his bottom lip, his eyes locked on Jack. "I'm really sorry if I hurt your feelings. You don't look all that bad. I mean, your head might look worse than mine did. But I'm sure you'll get better soon. I got to play ball again after about a week."

"No worries." Jack reached out, tugged at the bill of the boy's red baseball cap and offered up a smile. "You didn't hurt my feelings. And just so you know, I'm feeling better each day."

"It's good to see you up and around," Katie told Jack.

"Have we met?" he asked.

"Not really. I was here when you arrived, but you were pretty out of it."

Jack carried his mug to the coffee maker and poured a refill.

Katie chugged a glass of milk, then got up from the table and cleared the bowls, spoons and glasses from the table. "I hate to eat and run."

"Don't give it another thought. I've got this." Alana had no more than waved her off when the boys dashed to the mudroom, where they'd left a canvas bag and two bats. Once they'd gone outside, the back door slamming behind them, Jack took a seat at the table.

"You can have cereal for breakfast," Alana said, "but hotcakes are an option. I thought I'd scramble a couple of eggs for me. What sounds good to you?"

"Whatever you're having. Thanks." He took a sip of coffee. "Can I do anything to help?"

"No. I've got it all under control." She pulled bacon and a carton of eggs from the fridge. "Enjoy your coffee."

She'd no more than placed Grandpa Jack's cast iron skillet on the stove when Jack said, "So what's Katie's story? Have you been friends long?"

"I'll give you the short version. Katie was in college, studying to be a vet, when her mother died. Her stepdad had passed a few years earlier, so she took on custody of her two younger brothers. She'd gone back to school part-time, but money was tight, and then she got sick and had an appendectomy. When I found out she was about to be evicted from their apartment in town, I told her they could all stay here until she got back on her feet."

"That was nice of you."

She shook off his praise. "I had plenty of room here, so it seemed like the right thing to do."

"Still. Most people wouldn't do something like that. You have a big heart," he said.

Too big sometimes. "For what it's worth, Katie used to work for the vet in town. So she's been a huge help around here, especially with the mares. The only exercise they get is when she takes them for a ride or puts them out to pasture." Alana turned the fire down on the sizzling bacon, then pulled a bowl out of the cupboard. "And Mark and Jesse help, too. At least they try."

"I imagine the boys get underfoot sometimes."

"Not at all." Alana cracked four eggs into the bowl. "It's been great having them here. I used to be a nanny, and I love kids."

She reached into the cupboard drawer, pulled out a fork and began to whip the eggs.

"Any plans to have some of your own?"

She froze as she struggled with an answer. *Funny you should ask...*

Speaking of kids...

As if he'd seen her stiffen, sensed her hesitation and read into it, Jack said, "I'm sorry. That isn't any of my business."

Alana left the bowl on the counter and slowly turned to face him. "Actually, I was pregnant once and lost the baby. So your question threw me for a moment. But, yes, I'd love to have another child. And have a family of my own."

Her hand slid down the front of her, sculpting the small baby bump she kept hidden behind a baggy shirt. Catching herself, she turned away and reached for the bowl of raw eggs and, using the fork, began whipping them again.

She could feel Jack's eyes on her, so it didn't surprise her when he spoke. "Is that why you let people live with you?"

She didn't have many guests here—just four at the moment. But he had a point. So she turned again, facing him and the truth she rarely revealed. "I don't especially like living alone or not being a part of something bigger than me."

At that, he zeroed in on her. His gaze made her a little uneasy. But so what? She'd let him stay here, too.

"What happened to your family?" he asked.

Darn it. For a man who'd once claimed to be an attorney, he was beginning to sound like a shrink. But she'd kept enough secrets from him. "My mom died when I was just a baby, leaving me with my dad, who had a serious drug-and-alcohol problem. I wish I could say that's because he took my mother's death hard and was just trying to deal with the grief, but he was a big partyer. When I was seven, social services stepped in, and I was placed in foster care. A few months later, he died of an overdose."

Her thoughts drifted to the day she'd learned the facts of his death.

"He actually died on his friend's sofa. They were all pretty strung out, because it took his buddies a whole day to realize he hadn't moved in a while."

"I'm sorry." His tone, his compassionate gaze confirmed his words.

She gave a little shrug. "Not everyone has

a perfect childhood, but I survived. And even though it wasn't easy at the time, it all ended up okay. My last foster family lived down the street from Callie. You met her yesterday when we got back from the hospital."

"The pregnant blonde?"

"That's the one. She and I had a lot in common. Her parents had died, too, although she was only in foster care a year or so. Her great-aunt eventually took custody. And when I aged out of the system and had nowhere to go, Callie and her aunt invited me to live with them."

"So you've been friends since you were teenagers?"

"Yeah." A smile stole across her face. "You know, I've never had a problem making friends. But Callie's the best I've ever had. She's also the sister I never had."

Warmth surged through her heart, and grateful tears stung her eyes at the love and appreciation she had for Callie. She blinked back the faucet of emotion—as real as could be, but no doubt heightened by pregnancy hormones—and nodded toward the back door. "I'll tell you what. After breakfast, I'll take you out to the barn and introduce you to the horses."

"I'd like that," he said. "Thanks."

Good. Alana needed another subject to focus on. Topics like cowboys, ranches and livestock were much easier to handle than thoughts and memories that would only bring on tears.

"How many slices of bacon do you want?" she asked.

"Two, I guess. No, wait." A smile flickered on his face. "I think I like bacon. So make that three. Thanks."

As luck would have it, Jack remained pensive until breakfast was ready. She filled his plate with a good-size helping of scrambled eggs, three slices of bacon and buttered sourdough toast, then placed it in front of him.

She'd no more than returned to the table with her own meal when he finally spoke.

"When did your grandfather pass away?"

Her heart clenched, and another difficult topic came to mind. "He died in late December."

Right after Christmas. It had been a bitter-sweet holiday, yet special in its own way.

God, how she'd loved the man she'd barely had a chance to know.

"What was his name?"

"Jack," she said softly, her voice laden with the sweet memory.

He stopped chewing. "Seriously? His name was Jack, too?"

Her heart hammered its way out of her chest.

Jack picked up a crisp strip of bacon and lifted it to his mouth. "What a coincidence."

"Yes. Isn't it?" She pushed aside her plate and got to her feet, ready to bolt. "More coffee?"

"No, thanks. I'm okay for now."

Too bad she wasn't. And if she didn't confess about deceiving him soon, she might never be okay again.

Chapter Five

Why on heaven's earth had Alana lied about Clay's name being Jack?

And what if Clay found out that she'd given him Grandpa's last name, too?

Dumb. Just dumb.

Sure, she'd had her reasons at the time, but for each one that came to mind now, as sound and noble as it had seemed when she'd been at the hospital, reality shot it down.

There was just one way out. She needed to tell him the truth. That was a no-brainer. But each time she tried to come up with a way to broach the subject, the conversation began to play out in her mind, and she ended up feeling like a fool.

"We met one day and ended up in bed." *An easy lay, huh?*

"I didn't expect to get pregnant." *Not only an easy lay but a stupid one.*

"I actually liked you, but I left without telling you my name." *Not just easy and stupid, but impulsive, too. And foolish.*

No, the little chat they needed to have wasn't going to end well, no matter what kind of spin she tried to put on it.

Maybe when his memory returned, the conversation would flow organically. And when it did happen, he might take it better than she expected him to.

But what if he was the kind of man she'd thought he was, hoped he was? And what if, after learning that she'd lied to him, he decided he didn't want anything to do with her?

Worse yet, what if everything he'd told her in Colorado was true? If he was an attorney and had the money she thought he had, he had the means and know-how to seek joint custody. Or even…

She slowly shook it off.

"Just take things day by day," Grandpa Jack had told her. He'd been talking about running the ranch. But the words fit now, too. What would it hurt to wait another day or so?

In the meantime, as she led Jack out to the

stables, the two dogs bringing up the rear, she decided to continue playing it by ear.

Inside the barn, the morning sun peered through the dirty, smudged windows, creating a magical moment as glistening flecks of straw and dust danced in the air, not far from two saddles, each perched on a sawhorse. Mark and Jesse often came out to play on them, pretending to be cowboys.

When Alana and Jack reached the stabled mares, she pointed to the chestnut. "This girl is Bailey, and the black one is Selena."

Jack reached out and, after stroking each horse's neck, said, "They're good-looking horses."

Alana thought so, too. Not that she had any experience with that sort of thing. "Grandpa sold the geldings before he died, but he told me to hang on to the mares. I probably ought to sell them, but I have no idea how much they're worth. Either way, I kind of like having them around."

Jack spoke to the mares, much like Grandpa used to. "I'll bet you two would like to get outside for some exercise."

"Katie turns them out into the corral, and they seem to like that." Alana took a deep breath, savoring the barn scents of horse, leather and alfalfa. Grandpa used to smell like that sometimes, before he got really sick.

She moved toward a bale of alfalfa and reached for a handful to give Bailey and Selena a treat.

"Well, I'll be damned," Jack said. "I think you're pregnant."

Alana's gut clenched, her cheeks warmed to a slow burn. He knew. So much for her thinking she could put off that come-to-Jesus conversation they needed to have. She slowly turned to face him, ready to take her punishment. But Jack wasn't looking at Alana or at her silhouette. He was talking to Bailey while stroking her neck and examining her belly.

"Excuse me?" Alana asked.

"I'm not a vet, but I think Bailey's going to foal. I'd say in a month or so. When was she bred?"

She carefully let out a breath and willed the alfalfa in her trembling hand to still. "Grandpa tried to breed her right before he and I met. I think it was last fall. But he told me he didn't think it took. Then he got sick, and we were pretty busy with doctor's appointments and that sort of thing. But that had to be…" She began counting back the months. "That must have been in September. Maybe early October. I came a few days before Halloween, and he passed in December. Right after Christmas."

They'd shared two family holidays together— three, if you counted Halloween and the cookie-baking, pumpkin-carving night—all special times she'd never, ever forget.

"When's the last time the vet came out here?" Jack asked.

"I…" Alana was at a loss. "I don't know."

"You ought to schedule a call."

"Okay." She'd put it on her to-do list, although she had no idea what it would cost. Then again, the colt could be sold eventually. Grandpa's final gift.

But how could she sell Bailey's baby? It wouldn't seem right.

"Do you mind if I saddle Selena?" he asked. "We can take her out to the corral, and you can ride there until you feel more comfortable going out on the trail."

"I'd like that." A *lot*. Grandpa Jack would have liked the idea, too. He'd been working with her, hoping to help her feel comfortable on the horses before he'd gotten too sick to go outside. And it was sweet of Jack to offer.

As she handed half of the alfalfa to Bailey, Selena whinnied in jealousy. Bailey's head jerked back, causing Alana's heart to race, her grip on the hay to loosen enough that it dropped to the floor.

Jack placed a gentle hand on her shoulder, calming her with the warmth of his touch.

"Are you afraid of horses?" he asked. "If so,

we can work on it until you feel more comfortable around them."

We. She liked the sound of that. Yet as nice
as the offer was, as comforting the thought, she
took a step back and placed a shaky hand over
her small baby bump.

"I'm just a little jumpy," she said. "That's all."

But it was more than that. What if she fell off
or Selena stepped in one of the gopher holes and
stumbled?

No, Alana wouldn't risk it. She'd never do anything to hurt the baby she desperately wanted.
"Let's wait on the riding lessons, okay?"

"Why?"

She couldn't very well tell him the real reason.
And she wasn't about to tell him another lie she'd
have to confess to and apologize for. So she opted
for a different excuse that made perfect sense.
"You shouldn't overexert yourself until after your
appointment with Dr. Kirkland next week."

"You're probably right."

In this case, it was definitely the best decision. Unfortunately, when it came to Clay—also
known as Jack McGee—it appeared to be the
only good one she'd made since meeting him.

This morning, like he'd done the past four
mornings after he'd been discharged from the
hospital, Jack took a long, hot shower. While the

bathroom was still warm and steamy, he opened the door to cool it down. Then he wiped off the mirror and studied his face before shaving, trying to spot something familiar, anything that might spark a memory about the man he was and the life he'd led before coming to Rancho Esperanza.

He had a faint scar on his chin, one he vaguely remembered having for years. A dirt bike crash when he was just a kid came to mind, but the feeble thought disappeared as quickly as it surfaced.

On the upside, the swollen knot on his head had gone down considerably and the bruise under his eye had begun to yellow and fade. Even the stitches below his hairline had started to itch, a sign that the wound was healing.

This morning, when he'd stopped in the kitchen for a cup of coffee, Alana had reminded him about the appointment he had at the clinic on Tuesday to remove them, although he didn't need a reminder. As luck would have it, he didn't have a problem remembering anything that had happened during and since his stay at the hospital. That part of his memory was as clear as the blue Montana sky. But he'd be damned if he could recall anything prior to that time.

Of course, all wasn't lost. Over the past few days, he'd picked up on a few other things, like some abilities he must have acquired in the past. He had a decent grasp of the Spanish language.

And he had some definite preferences when it came to food and drink. He liked his eggs over easy, his coffee black and strong. He also had a hankering for prime rib and a baked potato—loaded with bacon, sour cream and chives.

Yesterday, while he'd been wandering around in the barn, he'd found an old beat-up radio on a shelf. He plugged the cord into an outlet on the wall and turned it on, just to see if it worked. It did. He didn't even have to touch the dial. It was tuned to a country station, and he recognized most of the songs.

On top of that, he seemed to know a lot about cattle and horses, which was a little surprising, considering the definitely citified clothing he'd been wearing at the hospital. But when it came to getting a bead on who he really was and where he'd come from, he still drew a blank.

But that didn't mean he sat around and stewed about the dilemma. He tried to keep himself busy by helping out around the ranch and trying to pay for his keep—more so today than ever.

"Don't forget I'm having Callie's baby shower here," Alana had said over breakfast.

"I won't."

His short-term memory worked just fine. But the fact that she tried so hard to help, to look after him, reached deep inside, as if filling a vast, emotional void he hadn't realized he had. But hell, why wouldn't it? Fate had knocked him off-kilter, and everything that held any real value to him seemed to be locked in one big black hole.

"I'll be serving lunch to the ladies around one," she told him as she placed a fruit salad into the fridge. "But I'll have plenty of food—enough for you to fix yourself a plate."

"Thanks. But if you don't mind, I'll just make a sandwich and take it with me. To be honest, I'd rather not be around when your friends get here."

She laughed, a pretty sound that lay easy on the ear and made him glad he'd drawn it out of her. "What's the matter? Are you afraid of crashing a hen party?"

"That's it, all right. They might unleash my inner rooster."

She laughed again, then gave him a playful sock on the arm. "Then, it's probably best if you make yourself scarce."

Damn. He liked seeing the playful side of her, the way her smile dimpled her cheeks and made her pretty green eyes light up.

And her laugh. He'd heard it before. He wasn't sure when, but the sound of it stirred an inner knowledge. It stirred his blood, too. And a memory seemed to rise up out of nowhere.

A hotel bar.

He'd walked in for a drink and spotted her, sitting alone, sipping a glass of wine.

Long wavy black hair tumbled over her shoulders. Big green eyes framed with thick, dark lashes. A light scatter of freckles across her nose. A bow-shaped mouth, pink and glossy after a fresh application of lipstick.

A burst of excitement, fueled by adrenaline, damn near torpedoed his heart, and...

The images drifted away as quickly as they had risen to the surface, but that same visceral reaction remained.

As his gaze locked on hers, her laughter faded as the humor seeped out of the room and something else took its place. If they'd met only once before, like she'd said, he'd bet a hundred bucks to a wooden nickel that their encounter hadn't been brief, that they'd done more than pass the time with idle chitchat. But he'd be damned if he could prove it. And he had no idea what to do about it now, when he wasn't at one hundred percent.

He nodded toward the mudroom. "I'm heading out to the barn. I might even take Selena for a ride this afternoon."

Oddly enough, she didn't suggest he wait until after he saw the doctor, as they'd agreed. Maybe it was *her* memory that was slipping— at least, the short-term portion. By the way her eyes widened, and her lips parted, he suspected her thoughts had drifted to that night, too. But he wasn't going to stick around and try to take a walk down memory lane with her when he had nothing more to go on than instant physical attraction.

The dogs seemed to have the same idea that he did, because they'd stuck by his side all morning and hung out while he ate one of the turkey sandwiches Alana planned to serve her guests. They'd also tagged along with him as he went into the barn, saddled Selena and then led her out into the yard.

After mounting the sturdy black mare, he spotted an old lady in the small orchard, wandering from tree to tree. A yellow scarf tied around her head held a shock of bright red curls at bay.

She wasn't very tall, barely over five foot one or two, and there was a spring in her step. She wore a green sweater, a brightly colored blouse boasting a butterfly print and blue stretch pants. He guessed her to be in her mid-to-late seventies.

What was she doing out there? Shouldn't she be inside, attending the baby shower with the other women?

His curiosity piqued, he remained in the yard and continued to watch her as she reached for a low-hanging cherry, plucked it from the branch and popped it into her mouth.

Didn't most women enjoy parties, luncheons and friendly chatter?

Unable to help himself, he rode to the small orchard to find out why she might be different.

At his approach, she looked up and lifted her free hand to shield the afternoon sun. Recognition brightened her eyes, and she smiled. "I see you found the Lazy M."

Did she know him? Or did she have him confused with someone else?

She furrowed her brow and eased closer, squinting as she approached him and the horse. "What in the hell happened to you? What'd you do? Say the wrong thing to a woman with a rolling pin in her hands?" She chuckled. "Looks to me like she smacked you upside the head."

He stiffened, and the mare took a sidestep. "Excuse me, ma'am?"

"Oh, don't mind me. I was just having fun with you. Other than taking a beating, Clay, how are you doin'?"

Clay? He'd been right. She was off her rock. Why else would she be wandering in the small orchard when all the other women were in the house? "My name's Jack."

She scrunched her craggy face, deepening the lines in her forehead. "That's not what you told me at the market. You bought yourself a water and asked for directions to the Lazy M. You said your name was Clay. I heard you, plain as day."

She was definitely an odd duck, but she still

had him stumped because some of what she said made sense.

She eyed him carefully. "You look dumbstruck."

That's because he was. "I'm sorry, ma'am. I don't remember meeting you."

"Are you kidding? I hope so, 'cause you'd better not get caught forgetting things around here." She nodded toward the house. "Some people might think you're touched in the head. Of course, I don't give a frog's leap when they say that about me. I use it to my advantage every chance I get. But you're too young and good-lookin' to let a rumor like that get out of hand."

So she admitted being a little…touched. And it sure seemed like it, but still…

"I see you're wearin' Jack's clothes," she said. "You workin' his ranch for his granddaughter?"

"Yeah. Sort of. For the time being, anyway."

She clicked her tongue. "I had you figured for a city slicker when I first saw you."

"You did, huh?" He tried to dig up the details of their supposed meeting, but all he got was a big fat blank.

"Dang, Clay. You look like a kid who just got told Santy Clause ain't real. You mean to tell me that you really *don't* remember?" She let out an unladylike snort. "I'll admit to being a little forgetful at times, although I'm not demented—no matter what my family might think."

He wasn't so sure about that.

She scanned the length of him, from the boots resting in the stirrups to the worn hat on his head. "I gotta say, you looked mighty fine in those fancy duds you were wearing, but sittin' up on that horse, dressed like a cowboy, is a better fit, if you ask me."

Jack sucked in a breath, then blew it out. "I'm sorry. This bump on my head has messed with my memory. What'd you say your name was?"

"I didn't. But I'm Betty Sue McInerny. You stopped by the casino, and I was playing on a slot machine."

She'd mentioned a market before. And now it was a casino? Maybe he'd seen her on two occasions, but it was just as likely that he'd been right in the first place and she'd gotten him confused with someone else.

Either way, he tried his best to remember her. She seemed vaguely familiar, but he still came up empty.

So what else was new?

"Aren't you supposed to be in the house?" he asked. "At the baby shower?"

"Yep. I'll go back in shortly. I just wanted to snatch a few cherries off the trees out here. When I was a little girl, my grandparents had an orchard. My recall isn't what it used to be these days, but some things are hard to forget. And when a special memory comes along, I like to indulge myself."

Jack could relate to that. He glanced up at the tree nearest him. "I see some ripe cherries. Let me pick some for you." He urged Selena forward, reached into the branches and plucked off a few. When Betty Sue neared him and the mare with up-stretched arms, he dropped them into her cupped hands.

She offered him a bright-eyed grin that suggested she might be more crafty than demented. "Thanks, Clay."

There it was again. *Clay.*

"Aunt Betty!" a woman called from the back porch. "Where'd you wander off to?"

"Oh, for Pete's sake." Betty rolled her green eyes and stuffed the fruit into her sweater pockets. "I can't even take a pee these days without my niece or nephew pounding on the door to make sure I'm okay." She turned toward the house, cupped her hands over her mouth and hollered, "I'll be right there, Carlene."

"You promise?" the woman retorted. "I don't want to have to get in the car and go looking for you again."

Betty let out a sigh, then turned to Jack, her head tilted upward, and blew out a raspberry.

"What'd I tell you? I can't even take a leisurely stroll without someone getting their panties in a wad."

Jack couldn't help but smile. He wasn't sure when he'd met the woman before or what he'd thought about her at the time, but he liked her now.

"I'll see you around, Clay." Then she headed toward the house.

Oddly enough, the name Clay seemed a little more familiar than Jack. But then again, poor Betty appeared to be half a bubble off plumb— a carpenter's term for being unbalanced or not quite straight. Just one more thing he seemed to know, a skill or knowledge he had, another small hint of who he was.

Either way, and as much as he hated to admit it, at this point in time, he couldn't rely on Betty Sue's memory any more than he could his own.

Alana carried a nearly empty pitcher of sweet tea into the kitchen to replenish it and spotted Marissa Garcia at the sink, washing dishes. Marissa, a pretty brunette in her midtwenties, had volunteered to help plan Callie's baby shower, but so far, she'd yet to join the other guests for more than a few minutes at a time. "Why don't you leave those for later. You're missing the party."

Marissa turned away from the sink and

grinned. "I will. I just thought I'd get a start on the clean-up."

"I appreciate all your help, decorating and cooking and all, but I was hoping you'd get a chance to spend some time hanging out with the rest of us."

Marissa was new in town—not that she hadn't had a chance to meet any of the locals. She worked part-time at the donut shop on Main and was also taking classes at the local junior college, where she hoped to get a business degree. It was a perfect career for her. She had a good marketing head on her shoulders. In fact, Marissa had encouraged Alana to prune the orchard, plant a big garden and then sell cherries, veggies and baked goods at the Fairborn Farmer's Market. It had been a super idea. And before long, Alana would begin to see money coming in rather than only going out.

"I'll be done here in a minute. Then I'll join you guys in the living room." Marissa tossed her a smile and winked. "Just in time for cake."

"Good! Because you did an amazing job with it. Who would have guessed you'd be not only a business whiz but a baker?"

Marissa laughed. "I guess you can say I'm a Jackie of all trades."

Jackie. *Jack*. Alana set the pitcher on the counter, then blew out a wobbly breath.

"Something wrong?" Marissa asked.

Alana hadn't gone into great detail about her pregnancy with her new friend, but Marissa knew that the father was a man Alana had met in a bar. And the revelation hadn't fazed her in the least. Probably because she was the kind of woman who didn't pass judgment. Instead, she seemed to be the kind who'd say, *Okay. So what're we going to do now?*

Normally, Alana would have shared her dilemma with Callie, but with twins on the way, a new man in her life and a wedding in her future, it might be best to let her BFF sit this one out. So she lowered her voice and told Marissa about Clay—or Jack. And the indecision she faced.

Marissa snatched the dish towel from the counter, dried her hands and let out a long, soft whistle.

"Any advice?" Alana asked her friend, who'd never been short on ideas.

"Why not take the doctor's advice and wait a little longer? It might be easier to talk to him once he remembers meeting you in Colorado."

Alana nodded. "That's what I was thinking. So I'm glad you agree." After letting out another little sigh, she retrieved ice cubes from the freezer.

"I've got a question for you," Marissa said. "Would you have any qualms about dating a man with children?"

"I love kids," Alana said. "Up until now, I didn't realize I'd have one of my own. So a man with children would appeal to me. I'd finally have the family I'd always wanted." Alana began to replenish the pitcher with sweet tea. "Why do you ask?"

"No real reason, I guess. It's just that I met this nice guy at the donut shop the other day. He's a single dad with two of the cutest little kids you ever saw."

"What's his name?"

Marissa chuckled. "I have no idea. But there were definitely sparks."

"So what's the problem?"

She took a deep breath, then slowly let it out. "My own experience with stepparents was horrible, and I'd hate to get involved in a complicated situation like that."

Before Alana could respond, Carlene Tipton entered the kitchen. "There you are, Alana. I'd been meaning to take you aside to share a bit of news you might like to know."

Carlene, as sweet and good-hearted as she was, had a tendency to gossip. And, unable to help herself, Alana took the bait. "What's that?"

Marissa cleared her throat, then took the pitcher from Alana. "I'll take this. That way, you two can have some privacy."

Alana doubted Carlene's "news" would be a

secret for long, but she appreciated Marissa's intuition and respect. "Thank you," she said, as she handed over the pitcher.

After Marissa left the room, Carlene folded her arms across her chest. "You remember Adam Hastings?"

How could she forget? The rich Texan was hell-bent on buying Rancho Esperanza, even though Alana had refused to sell—to him or anyone. "What about him?"

"I heard he made another offer on the Circle R. And this time, Paul Clemmons accepted it."

"That's good... Right?" Maybe now he had enough Montana property to back off and leave Alana alone.

"Good for Paul, I suppose. But some folks wonder why Hastings is so interested in buying up property here."

Something deep inside, that same disconcerting feeling Alana got whenever she was about to be removed from a foster home and transported to another, rose up, insisting that "some folks" might have good reason to be suspicious.

When Jack was sure the baby shower had ended and all the guests had left the ranch, he returned to the house and washed up in the mudroom. Just beyond the doorway to the kitchen, he heard the refrigerator door open and shut.

"Is that you, Jack?" Alana called out.

"Yeah. It's me." Whoever "me" was. He turned off the faucet, reached for the towel hanging near the sink and dried his hands.

When he entered the kitchen, he paused for a moment and watched Alana as she put away the last of the party leftovers. She wore a loose yellow sundress, and her hair was pulled up into a messy topknot, revealing a pair of pearl earrings, small and simple yet lending her an elegance that...

His leisurely assessment and admiration stalled, and his smile faded. Had he seen them before today? Had he noticed the delicate earrings that added to her pretty face?

When nothing came to mind, he shook off the feeling of déjà vu and asked, "Is the coast clear?"

"Yes, and a good time was had by all." She turned to face him, blessing him with a smile. "It's safe for you to come home."

Home. A couple of days ago, that word might have sent him scurrying for a memory. But now it just sounded...nice.

"It's pretty quiet around here," he said. "Where are the boys?" Come to think of it, he hadn't seen them since breakfast.

"One of their friends, a boy on their ball team, invited them over for a playdate. So Katie dropped them off before the shower started. She just left to pick them up."

He and Alana were alone?

His hormones stirred, and the fog in his brain shifted slightly, allowing a break in the clouds and a spot of clarity.

An attractive brunette sitting alone at a small, candlelit table, lifting a glass of red wine to her lips.

Recognition shot through him. *Alana.*

Something else stirred, too.

Awareness. *Heat.*

The brief piece of memory vanished. Poof. Dissipating into his fog-shrouded brain.

He blinked as he tried to re-create it, to latch on to it somehow, but it was gone for now, leaving him completely at a loss. Yet the sexual awareness remained, and his gaze locked on hers.

Her eyes filled with worry, and she closed the distance between them. "Is something wrong?"

"I'm not sure, but I think—"

She placed a gentle hand on his bicep, and his muscle flexed in response. Her citrusy scent, her sweet touch, those expressive green eyes… The memory may have disappeared, but the sexual yearning, the sense that they'd shared more than smiles remained, filling the room, invading his senses.

"What happened just now?" She removed her

hand from his arm and took a step back. "Did you remember something?"

"Yeah. I think so." He sucked in a deep breath, then blew it out. "Where, exactly, did we meet?"

Her face paled, and her lips parted. "I…told you. We met in Colorado."

"That part I know. But…" Damn. Why couldn't he pull up any more recollections of that day?

No, it was nighttime. There was a candle on the table.

"You told me we met in a bar," he said. "Was it in the evening?"

She bit down on her bottom lip, then she nodded slowly. "Yes. Like I told you before, I'd attended a cattle symposium, and at the end of the day, I decided to have a drink before dinner."

"Wine, right? I think it was red."

Again, she nodded.

"And I joined you at your table." It wasn't a question. Somehow, he just knew that's how it happened.

Alana stared at the floor for several beats, then she looked up and caught his eye. "Yes, you approached me."

She must have let him sit with her. "What happened that night?"

"I… We…" She folded her arms across her chest. "I shouldn't force you to remember things."

"I think I'm ready now. I keep getting some

fleeting thoughts about that evening. I just want you to help me connect them. Did we end up on good terms?"

"To be completely honest, I'm not sure."

He wiped a hand over his face. Something must have gone wrong, but Alana wasn't being much help. Betty Sue said he'd asked for directions to the Lazy M. So he'd obviously been on his way to see her. But four months later? That didn't make sense, even in his fuzzy state.

"Why did I come looking for you?" he asked.

"I really don't know." She inched away.

"You must have an idea. Why would I show up after four months? You know more than you're telling me, don't you?"

"I'm just following doctor's orders. Remember? It's best if we let your memory return naturally. I don't want to force it."

Okay, then. Maybe he'd do the forcing. Let's see if his gut feeling was true.

He moved forward, backing her against the counter, his eyes locked on hers. He lifted his hand to cup her jaw. His thumb brushed her cheek, stroking it. Caressing it.

Her lips parted, and he could see it in her eyes. There'd been chemistry the night they'd met, and that hadn't changed. Something told him that's why he came looking for her, but was he the type of guy who impulsively followed his animal instincts? Did his hormones rule?

No, she was attractive, but this wasn't merely about lust.

He let his hand fall, and he shuffled back. "There was more to our meeting in Colorado." He knew it, sensed it. He'd read it in her eyes just a heartbeat before, but something shifted. Now all he spotted was...what? Guilt? Fear? Uneasiness?

He couldn't quite put his finger on exactly what it was, but she was clearly holding out on him.

Why? She might say it's because the doctor hadn't wanted her to push him too hard, but he sensed it was more than that.

Betty Sue might seem a little...off, but she'd seemed pretty sure of herself. *That's not what you told me at the market. You bought yourself a water and asked for directions to the Lazy M. You said your name was Clay. I heard you, plain as day.*

Was that true?

There was only one way to find out. He'd have to do a little pushing himself. "Are you sure my name's Jack?"

Her eyes widened and her lips parted, validating his suspicion. "W-why do you ask?"

He folded his arms across his chest and pressed on. "Because I think it might be Clay."

Chapter Six

Alana's heart sank to the pit of her stomach. Clay knew something, although she had no idea what. Enough to know she'd lied to him. Or at least to suspect it.

Are you sure my name's Jack? Because I think it might be Clay.

That wasn't the only question in his eyes demanding an honest answer—and a confession.

She placed her hand over her baby bump, as if she could protect the little one from its father's questioning expression. Or maybe she was trying to protect herself—and the seven-year-old child she used to be, the one who'd faced a frustrated foster parent after she'd wet the bed on the first night of her placement and felt compelled to run out of the room before she crumpled into one big hot mess at his feet.

Yet while trembling inside, the teenager who'd toughened up over the years demanded that she lift her head high, stand firm and stick to her story. "You didn't say much that night, and I wasn't sure how much of what you were saying was true."

At that, he stiffened. "You thought I was lying to you?"

She hadn't known what to think. And if truth be told, once he offered her a charming smile, her alcohol-laced brain had turned to mush, and she hadn't done much thinking at all.

"You were a stranger in a bar. I was a woman alone, and a long way from home." She shrugged. "I thought you may have said your name was Jack, but now that you mention it, your name could have been Clay. But even then, I wasn't sure."

His brow furrowed, as if her words had somehow wounded him. "Why would you question my honesty?"

Her cheeks warmed and her heart soared up from her belly and nearly jumped out of her chest. What in the world was she supposed to say now? *We had a one-night stand. It didn't mean anything.*

If their past had been a movie or a book, the tagline might read "Gorgeous man with money walks into an upscale bar and meets a financially strapped woman who has been craving love, intimacy and security her entire life."

The rest of the story would pretty much play out on its own. They drink too much, and she suggests sex.

How would that explanation play out in his mind?

Badly, she suspected, because right now, it wasn't playing out very well in hers. But even though she hated to lay it all out on the table, she'd promised herself there'd be no more lies.

"I did most of the talking that night," she said, "and you were a good listener. I'm afraid your last name never came up at all."

"And you never thought to ask?"

"I wish I had, but I didn't."

And that was the pure, unadulterated truth. Even in an alcohol-laced buzz, she could see that they were clearly mismatched in terms of their education and socioeconomic backgrounds. And after they'd made love, as amazing as it had been, as beautiful as she'd felt, she'd sobered like Cinderella the moment the clock began to chime. Then she'd reverted to her default mode—a barefoot, rag-clad woman who knew where she belonged—and where she didn't. So she'd escaped before the magical night had ended.

Besides, men like Clay rarely asked her out a second time.

Although there had been one.

Bradley Lewis Thomason. She'd dated him for two months, and he'd treated her well. Nice restaurants, fine dining. A couple of shows where they had front-row seats.

When the holidays had rolled around, she'd asked him if she would finally get to meet his family. He'd shrugged, then he'd changed the subject. When she'd pressed him, he'd told her that she wasn't the kind of girl his parents expected him to date.

His cool response, the reality of their differences, had hurt. She might have been crushed completely if she hadn't thrown a glass of wine in his face before walking out the door.

That pride-shattering experience had taught her that she shouldn't entertain foolish dreams about any kind of relationship, let alone marriage, to a wealthy man with status and connections.

"Seriously?" Clay asked, as he slowly closed the distance between them. "That's all you can tell me about that night? About the conversation we had?"

That's pretty much all she wanted to tell him, but he deserved to know the truth about his identity, even though she had very little to offer him in that respect.

"You were well dressed and polite," she said. "You mentioned that you lived in Texas. But that's about it."

"No, Alana. There was more to it than what you've told me. We had sex that night, didn't we?"

It was an easy assumption for him to make, and as much as she'd like to deny it, she couldn't.

"Yes, we did. I was too embarrassed to admit that. I'm not the kind of woman who would go to bed with a man I'd just met. But I did that night. And so I slipped out of your hotel room while you were asleep."

Yet he'd managed to find her. Had she somehow left a glass slipper behind?

Clay raked a hand through his hair, and his brow furrowed. "Damn. Was it that bad, Alana?"

Bad? Making love with him? "Oh, no! It wasn't that. It was good. Great, actually. It's just that… I don't know." Her cheeks burned, no doubt turning a fire-engine red. She almost flapped her hand in front of her face to cool herself down, but that would only fan the flames. Darn it. She'd really stepped in it now.

"Then," he said, "if the sex was that good, why didn't you wake me up and tell me goodbye?"

"Because…" She sucked in a fortifying breath

and blew it out. "Well, assuming you actually lived in Texas, that's a long way from Montana. I knew better than to expect more than what we'd just shared and assumed we'd never see each other again."

"Yet here I am."

Yes, here he was. "And that fact brings up a few questions in my mind, too. But until your memory returns, I can't even ask you why—or how—you found me."

"You have a point there. So is that all you have to tell me?"

"Pretty much. In a nutshell. You also mentioned being an attorney, but… Well, you have to admit that people aren't always honest with each other when they meet in a bar."

"Voice of experience?"

Heat blasted her cheeks again. "No! That was a first for me. A one-night thing. I don't make a habit of picking up men in bars and giving them a line of BS. But I've heard other people do that. And just for the record, I didn't tell you anything about me that wasn't entirely true. I…" She'd begun to ramble. In fact, so much so, that even she found her story hard to believe.

"So that's it?" he asked again, his voice laden with frustration. "All you can tell me is that I might be a Texas attorney named Jack or Clay Something-or-other?"

She could tell him that she'd conceived a baby that night, but now wasn't the time to lay something that heavy on him. Obviously, he could hardly wrap his mind around the meager details she'd just given him. So she merely nodded.

He blew out a heavy sigh, then scrubbed his face.

Sympathy welled in her heart and began to fill her eyes. She could apologize, but she also valued self-preservation.

She straightened her shoulders and lifted her chin. "Hey. I didn't invite you here. Not that you aren't welcome. But I have no idea why you're in Montana. And apparently, you don't, either."

His demeanor softened. "You're right."

Before she could conjure a response or any further explanation, her cell phone rang. Talk about being saved by the bell.

She crossed the small kitchen and snatched the outdated phone charging on the counter as if it were a lifeline and glanced at the screen.

Ramon Cruz. Callie's husband. Why would he be calling her? Probably to thank her for throwing the shower. She should let it roll over to voice mail and then continue the conversation she'd been having with Clay, but she was more than ready for a break. So she swiped her finger across the screen and took the call. "Hey, Ramon. What's up?"

"Callie thinks she's in labor. She's having some contractions, so we're meeting her obstetrician at the hospital."

"Oh, no." Alana gripped the phone tight. It was too early. Six weeks or more. Anything could go wrong, especially with a twin birth. "I'll meet you guys there. I mean, I won't barge in on you, but I…"

"Alana. Don't give it another thought. Callie wants you with us."

Of course she did. That's what friends were for. When Callie had given birth to Micah, her firstborn, Alana had been there. And Callie had been there the next year, when Alana had lost her first baby.

Her hands trembling, Alana ended the call. Then she turned to Clay. "I need to go to the hospital. Callie's in labor. Early. We'll talk later."

"Sure." He nodded toward the door leading to the living room and the rest of the house. "Get ready and grab whatever you'll need. I'll drive you."

She would have declined his offer, but her head was spinning and her heart was racing like a stock car driver barreling his way to the finish line. So she shouldn't drive herself. Why risk a speeding ticket or an accident?

On top of that, she had the health and safety of her own baby to consider.

"Okay. Thanks, Clay. I'll grab my purse."

"Better throw some things into an overnight bag. This could take a while."

Alana was so focused on rushing to her friend's bedside that they'd gotten nearly ten miles down the road before something about Clay's comment struck an odd chord in her mind.

How would he know that this might take a while? Did he have experience with a woman in labor?

The old ranch pickup bumped and chugged along the country road that led to the hospital in Kalispell. Other than the noise of the engine that needed a tune-up, silence filled the cab.

Clay had plenty of questions he wanted to ask, but the worry etched across Alana's face and the way she wrung her hands in her lap stopped him from even broaching the conversation they'd had earlier.

Instead, he told her about the leak he'd spotted in the pump that supplied water to the pasture where the few cattle she had left grazed.

"It's not a bad one," he said, "but it'll need to be fixed. And I also found some loose fence posts along the edge of the property in the south forty."

She let out a groan, then gave her shoulders a roll. "I've finally been able to pay Grandpa's back taxes, but no matter what I do or what repairs I make, my to-do list continues to get longer."

It went without saying that the costs of getting the ranch up and running again continued to grow, too. Clay shot a glance across the seat to where Alana sat gazing out the passenger window as the countryside drifted by.

"Those repairs don't need to be made today," he said. "You can put them off for a while. But I wouldn't wait too long. That leak is only going to get worse."

"I know what you must be thinking," she said. "I've heard it before from the guy who wants to buy the ranch. He told me to take the money he offered and buy a new house in town."

That wasn't a bad idea, although he sensed he'd better keep that thought to himself. "It's not like you have to repair everything at once."

At that, she turned toward him, her eyes filled with a different kind of worry. "How much do you think it'll take to fix the pump and replace those posts?"

"Actually, I made a mental note of the parts you'll need. Since I can fix them myself, it shouldn't cost more than four or five hundred dollars."

He turned down the road toward town. Hey. How about that? He may not know who in the hell he really was, but it appeared that he was a bilingual attorney who knew his way around a ranch and wasn't a stranger to mechanical know-how and hard work. That was nice, he supposed, but a lot of good it did him when he couldn't seem to remember anything else.

He shot a glance at the beautiful brunette who sat next to him. She'd admitted that they'd had a one-night stand. Had they actually been strangers? Did she know more about him than she'd shared?

As they continued along the road to the hospital, an elephant the size of Texas sat between them. He did his best to ignore it, and she seemed to be doing the same thing. Then again, maybe she was so worried about her friend that she couldn't be bothered with anything else.

He turned on the radio, which had been preset to a country station that played classic hits. It didn't take him very long to realize he knew most of the songs. He didn't know what that meant in the scheme of things. But if he was from Texas, as Alana had said, it made sense.

In spite of the music that filled the cab, Clay grew increasingly uneasy, and by the time they neared the hospital entrance, his clammy, cold hands clenched the steering wheel, his heart rate had spiked and he felt compelled to bolt.

Bad things happened at hospitals. People died. Kids were left alone and confused… Scared. Heartbroken.

Now, there was one flicker of a memory that he wasn't eager to remember.

Still, he pulled into the circular drop-off area and stopped to let Alana out in front of the lobby door.

She reached for the handle, but before opening it, she turned to him and offered a faint yet appreciative smile. "Thanks for driving me."

"No problem. I'll park the truck, then I'll hang out in the lobby."

"You don't need to do that," she said. "I can catch a ride home. Somehow."

Clay wasn't about to leave her here. What if something went wrong during the birth? That happened sometimes. He wasn't entirely sure how he knew that. He just did.

"It doesn't matter," he said. "Go on inside and find Callie. I'll be sitting in the lobby waiting area if you need me."

Alana tucked a strand of hair behind her ear. "It could be a long time."

"I know." It could take days. And it didn't always end up well.

But how did he know that?

Another memory stirred in his mind like the start of a small dust storm. A dark one, it seemed. One he didn't think he'd want to revisit.

As she began to shut the passenger door, he stopped her. "I need a way to reach you. Give me your cell phone. You can borrow Callie's or Ramon's to send me a text and keep me updated."

She reached into her purse, pulled out her iPhone, an old version that had seen better days, and handed it to him. Then, after shutting the pickup door, she hurried to the entrance.

Clay remained there for a moment, the engine idling, as the thought of a young boy walking out of a similar place, his heart pounding, palms sweating, burst onto the mental scene. Fear scurried up and down his spine until something—God only knew what—chased the recollection away.

When another vehicle pulled up behind him, he removed his foot from the brake and went in search of a parking space. Once he found one, he headed toward the hospital entrance, his steps slow. Hesitant. Bothered by a memory that refused to rise up from the depths.

He'd no more than stepped into the lobby when his sense of uneasiness grew into a realization that smacked him between the eyes. He hated hospitals. He wasn't sure how he knew that for a fact, but he did.

Had he felt the same way when Alana had brought him here last week? Or had he been too out of it to realize where he was—or to remember why he'd rather be anyplace than here?

It didn't matter. He sucked in a deep breath, then pushed through his fear and apprehension.

He was here for Alana. And he'd stick it out for as long as it took.

As it turned out, he'd had to wait only an hour when the first text came through. The caller ID indicated that Callie was sending the message, although it must be from Alana.

So far, so good. The doctor ordered medication to stop labor. It seems to be working.

Clay typed.

Sending good thoughts.

An hour later, another text came through.

Callie is resting easy. Hungry?

Clay hated hospital food—another oddball memory that seemed to be connected to the last.

Yes. Here? Or can we go somewhere else?

She replied.

I think the Mulberry Café is still open. OK?

Anything was better than here. So he agreed. Before he could slip the cell phone into his pocket, a new text chimed, from Fairborn Medical Center.

You have an appointment with Dr. Patel at our office Wednesday at 9:00 AM.

A checkup? he wondered. Probably. Not any of his business, he supposed. So he shrugged it off and waited for Alana to come downstairs.

Moments later, she stepped out of the elevator with a tall dark-haired man who appeared to be in his late twenties.

"Clay," Alana said, "this is Ramon Cruz, Callie's husband. Ramon, this is my friend, Clay."

The two men shook hands, their grips firm.

"The contractions have stopped," Alana said, "but the doctor wants to keep her overnight."

"I'm glad to hear that." Another odd sensation settled over him like a cool, dark mist. Was it another memory? Or was it a premonition? Did he get those kinds of things?

"I'm going to spend the night here," Ramon said, "but since Callie just dozed off and should sleep for a while, I thought I'd join you guys."

Clay didn't have a problem eating a meal with Ramon, but he wished he could reach for his wallet and whip out a hundred dollar bill or a credit card. He liked paying his own way. But unfortunately, ever since the accident—which seemed more likely to be a mugging and carjacking—he didn't have any cash on him.

As if sensing Clay's dilemma, Ramon said,

"Don't either of you even think about paying for dinner. It'll be my treat tonight. Besides, I owe you for throwing Callie's baby shower."

"You don't owe me a thing," Alana said. "But I appreciate the offer. Besides, I don't get into town very often. And I love the Mulberry Café, especially the sweet treats Callie used to bring home to me."

As they all turned toward the glass doors that led outside, Clay couldn't help gazing at Alana, and not just her pretty face. He scanned the length of her and back. She was a shapely woman, even in those baggy clothes she seemed to favor.

Not that it mattered to him. And it certainly didn't take away from her appearance. Yet as she placed her hand on her belly, as she caressed it, he nearly stopped dead in his tracks.

Was that a baby bump?

If so, was it a result of their one-night stand?

Ramon's late-model SUV beat the old ranch pickup to the café, but by only a couple of minutes. Alana suspected Ramon wanted to have a quick dinner so he could get back to the hospital, and she didn't blame him. He clearly loved Callie and would want to be with her if she should wake up and need him. Ramon knew he hadn't actually fathered the twins, but as far as he was concerned, those babies were his.

As Alana and Clay neared the café entrance, they spotted a small, scruffy-haired black dog sitting on its haunches next to the oak-slatted, wrought iron bench to the left of the door. Someone had given it water in a disposable cup and a paper plate with what appeared to be a cheeseburger broken into pieces. At their approach, the little thing stopped munching and looked up at them, doe-eyed and apprehensive.

It didn't have a collar or tags, so Alana assumed it was a stray, although someone had clearly provided it with an evening meal.

Clay stopped and reached down to give the mutt a scratch behind its floppy ears. "How're you doin', buddy? You look a little puny." He straightened, turned his attention to Alana and gave a little shrug. "I guess you could say I'm an animal lover."

"Clearly." She'd already reached that obvious conclusion. The ranch dogs had taken to him right away, and he was good with the horses, too.

Clay glanced at the blue-and-white-striped awning that sheltered the eatery's door and surveyed the entrance. "So this is the Mulberry Café?"

"Yep. This is it. Callie went to work here right after she arrived in town. She quit when she and Ramon got married last month. It's probably not the kind of restaurant you're used to, but it's a favorite of the Fairborn locals."

"I hope I didn't come across as a snob," he said.

"You didn't." Back in that Colorado bar, he'd not only been well dressed but he'd been well mannered, too. And he'd left a generous tip for the cocktail waitress.

"Is this where Callie met Ramon?" he asked.

Alana nodded. "He'd gone through a divorce a few months earlier and had been eating most of his meals in various restaurants around town. But most of them were here at the café. The food is really good."

"I don't doubt it." Clay chuckled. "But I'll bet Ramon enjoyed the service more than the menu."

A smile broke across her face, the first real one she'd had since Clay had arrived at the ranch. "You're right."

Clay opened the door for her, and she walked inside. When he'd joined her, she pointed to the left of the cash register where a refrigerated case displayed a variety of desserts. "They look good, don't they?"

"They sure do."

"Gloria, the cook, has worked here for years. She's a whiz in the kitchen, but she's a darn good baker, too. Her pies are to die for. And so is her chocolate-mousse cake."

Clay nudged Alana's arm, then pointed to the table where Ramon sat.

Ramon waved them over. They'd no more than started across the café to join him when his cell phone rang. He glanced at the display, then took the call, which wasn't a surprise. The busy town councilman was preparing for the upcoming election. He also coached a Little League team that had done so well it had gone on to compete in the county-wide All-Stars Tournament.

He had a lot going on in his life these days, but he'd made it clear that nothing was more important to him than his new wife and family.

As Clay pulled out a chair for Alana, Ramon got to his feet. "Go ahead and order. I need to take this call, but I'll do it outside. I'll be back in a few."

Alana took a window seat that provided her with a view of Elmwood Drive, which had very little traffic at this time of the evening. Then she reached for one of the menus sitting on the table.

The café door creaked open as Ramon went out, and a small black blur made a mad dash inside and ran right up to Shannon McIntire, the college student who waited tables part-time, just as she was placing a plate in front of an older man seated by himself.

A big grin spread across her face. "Hey, Blackie. You're not supposed to come in here.

You're gonna get me into big-time trouble if Gloria sees you."

Shannon might wear the typical uniform of the other employees—a scoop-neck white T-shirt with a Mulberry Café logo on the chest—but with her short black hair, the ends tinted pink tonight, and a couple of eyebrow piercings, she stood out from the others. She was also Gloria's niece.

"Dammit!" Gloria rushed out of the kitchen. "What did I tell you about feeding that stray mutt, Shannon? You want the health department to shut us down?"

"I'm sorry, Gloria."

"Sorry won't cut it if we have to board up the windows and find another way to pay the rent. Take that dog outside and wash your hands. I'm going to call Animal Control."

Moments later, after returning from the ladies' restroom, Shannon made her way to the table where Alana sat with Clay and pulled her pad and pencil from the front pocket of her apron. "Sorry about that." She glanced first at Alana, then she gave Clay an appreciative once-over. "I've never seen you before. You new in town?"

"Just visiting."

"Cool. Always nice to meet a friend of Alana's." She nodded toward the restaurant door. "That little black puppy is a real sweetheart. I'd take her home in a heartbeat, but I live with

Gloria. And she's allergic to pet dander. At least that's what she says each time I ask to adopt a stray. But once I graduate and get a place of my own, I'll get as many dogs and cats as I want."

Alana bit down on her bottom lip, then peered out the window at the poor dog.

Clay chuckled. "Don't tell me. It's written across your face. I know what you're thinking."

He was right. Alana turned to Shannon. "Tell Gloria not to waste her time on a phone call. I'm taking that dog back to the ranch with me."

"Awesome!"

Before Shannon could hightail it back to the kitchen, Ramon returned to their table and handed her a couple of twenties. "I'm afraid I can't stay, but I'm springing for Alana and Clay's dinner tonight."

"Is something wrong?" Alana asked, ready to ditch her dinner plans if Callie needed her.

"No," Ramon said. "Micah just called to let me know he picked up a couple of carne asada burritos at Don Juan's Cantina and is taking them back to the hospital, so I'm going to join him."

"Oh, my gosh!" Shannon slapped a hand to her chest, her fingers splayed, blue polish chipped. "Did Callie have her babies?"

"Not yet," Ramon said. "It was just a false alarm. She's going to have to spend the night, but she can go home in the morning."

"Oh, that's a relief." She slowly lowered her hand. "I talked to Micah a couple of days ago, and he said she still had a month or two to go."

"Micah?" Clay asked, a splash of confusion crossing his brow.

"Technically, he's Callie's son," Ramon explained. "But as far as I'm concerned, Micah is ours. He's in town for the summer and doing an internship at the hospital blood bank, so he's been slipping in and out of the lab to check on his mom."

"He's amazing," Alana added. "I hope you get a chance to meet him. He's only sixteen, but he's going to graduate from Baylor University in December. Then he's off to medical school."

"Wow," Clay said. "Smart kid."

"And a good one," Alana said. "I've loved him since the day he was born."

"I hate to run off," Ramon said, "but I don't want to keep Micah waiting."

"I don't blame you." Clay stretched his arm across the seat back of the empty chair beside him. "Thanks for picking up the tab. Next time, dinner's on me."

So he was fair and generous. Nice to know. But he'd have to get a job that paid more than just room and board. Or else his memory would need to return so he could access a bank account.

"It's a deal." Ramon turned toward the door.

"Hey, Mr. Cruz," Shannon called out, stopping him. "Tell Callie that I love kids and will be happy to babysit for you guys anytime."

"Will do." Ramon winked, then pulled open the door and stepped onto the sidewalk.

Clay pushed his chair back, got to his feet, reached into the front pocket of his jeans and pulled out the keys to the pickup.

Alana furrowed her brow. "Where are you going?"

He nodded toward the door. "Since it sounds like you're dead set on saving that stray dog's furry butt, I'd better go get her and put her into the pickup. Something tells me Gloria might make that call anyway."

Alana's heart warmed. "You don't mind doing that for me?"

He tossed her a charming grin, one just like the many he'd given her the night they'd met. "I'll be back in a flash—unless that little dog doesn't want to be adopted."

Alana studied Clay as he crossed the diner, taken by his sexy, cowboy swagger.

So who was this guy? Fancy lawyer or down-home ranch hand?

Was he one of the good guys—bright, successful and decent? Or just slick and charming?

The jury was still out, she supposed. The only thing certain was that he stirred a feeling inside of her that she'd never felt before. Not since the night they'd made love.

She'd blamed a combination of lust and one too many glasses of merlot for lowering her guard, for suggesting they make love. But she hadn't had a drop of alcohol since, and yet tonight, she was still sorely tempted to suggest they wrap up this evening by having a glass of wine and…

No. She wouldn't do that again. Not until they both knew exactly who Clay actually was.

But when she glanced out the window and saw him gently scoop the stray into his arms, whispering something to the bundle of fur as he carried it to the pickup and placed it inside the cab, warmth filled her heart with a hot-fudge-sundae sweetness. And for some dumb reason, his true identity no longer seemed to matter.

Chapter Seven

On the way back to the ranch, Alana held the floppy-eared black cocker mix in her lap. Every now and then, it squirmed in her arms, but only to give her hand or her cheek an appreciative lick.

"Aren't you a little sweetheart? All you need is a bath and a full tummy."

"Looks like you found a new buddy," Clay said.

"So it seems." She had no idea what she was going to do with three dogs, but there was no way she would have left it to fend for itself on the streets, especially when Gloria had threatened to call Animal Control.

She shot a glance across the seat at Clay, who was gazing at the road ahead.

He was a handsome man—more so than anyone had a right to be. But more important than that, he was one of the good guys. Kind, thoughtful… sweet. At least she hoped her assumption about him was right. She still wasn't sure what he was doing in Montana—or what had happened to him. Car accident? A crime victim? They should probably report it to the sheriff, but they couldn't very well do so when they had zero details and only a hunch.

She shot a glance across the seat at Clay, who was proving to be a friend.

"Thank you," she said.

He turned, and his head tilted slightly. "For what?"

"Driving me to the hospital this afternoon. Waiting for me—" she looked down at the scraggly mutt "—and for helping me rescue this sweet little girl."

He blessed her with a dimpled grin. "You clearly have a heart for strays, whether they have four legs or two. The way I see it, that little mutt and I are both lucky to have crossed your path."

"You're not a stray," she said. "You have a home. A life. You just don't know where. Yet."

"That may be true, but I sure feel pretty damned lost and homeless right now."

She didn't doubt that. And until he remembered who he was and where he lived, all he had was her.

"You'll get your memory back in time," she said, hoping that by making that claim out loud it would come to pass. "But until then, you're welcome to stay with me as long as you want."

"I appreciate that."

And she appreciated *him*. For his kindness—not just to her but to Katie, Mark and Jesse, even though they seemed to spend more time off the ranch than on it. She also appreciated his help with the repairs. And above all else, she was especially thankful for the baby he'd given her.

Clay nodded toward the dog sitting in her lap. "What are you going to call her?"

Alana hadn't given it much thought. "Blackie comes to mind, but that's too... Well, it's not very unique. Maybe Licorice. What do you think?"

"Sounds good to me."

They continued on in silence. A couple of times, she opened her mouth to speak, then thought better of it.

Rather than make idle chatter, she reached for the dial on the dash and turned on the radio, which was preset to a country-western station. An Alan Jackson love song was playing softly, lulling her into a pensive yet romantic mood. She leaned back in her seat, closed her eyes and allowed her memories to take her back to the night she met Clay in Colorado.

She'd been sitting alone and sipping a glass of wine at a small table in the upscale hotel bar. She hadn't been looking for company. Instead, she was contemplating what she'd learned at the symposium and evaluating the cost she'd paid to attend against the benefits. Then a handsome guy wearing a designer suit had approached wearing a friendly grin.

"Mind if I join you?"

She'd looked up at him, surprised by the interruption—yet swept away by it, too. After a heart-spinning beat, she returned his smile and pointed to the chair across from hers.

"Sure. Have a seat."

The encounter had been magical from the start, and she'd found herself opening up to him in unexpected ways. After an hour or so, it had seemed only natural for her to reach across the table and place her hand on his.

"I know we'll never see each other again, but I've enjoyed meeting you, Clay. And I'm feeling very much alone right now."

He'd seemed surprised at her implication, yet pleased by it, too.

Would he ever remember that night, too? Not just their surreal first meet, but their magic they'd shared in bed?

She cut another glance across the seat, where Clay sat, his hands on the wheel, eyes on the road ahead. He seemed to be lost in his thoughts, too. But he wasn't smiling.

She suspected he was pondering the frustrating situation he found himself in, thanks to the accident he'd had—or whatever violent incident in which he'd been involved. She nearly broached the subject of that amazing night in Colorado, but she let it go.

Until he had a better grasp on who he was or what had happened to him, there wasn't much to say, other than conjecture and a lot of what-ifs.

Of course, she had her own reasons for keeping quiet on the drive home, too. Her thoughts and memories were too special, too heart stirring. And, if truth be told, they were too heated to forget.

As the pickup pulled into the yard, Rascal and Chewie trotted out of the barn with tails wagging, barking out to welcome them home.

Alana opened the passenger door and, with Licorice in her arms, greeted the dogs. "Hey, guys. Chill. I brought you a new friend."

Licorice didn't seem too sure about that claim, as she nuzzled into Alana's chest, apprehensive of the unfamiliar surroundings and the two dogs who appeared more eager to meet her than she was to meet them.

"They're not going to hurt her," Clay said. "Just set her down and let them get to know each other."

He was probably right. Alana bent and placed Licorice on the ground, and before long, the three dogs were sniffing each other and running around like newly acquainted fur buddies.

"See? What'd I tell you?" Clay placed a gentle hand on Alana's back in a sweet, affable gesture, but it sent an unexpected tingle of warmth straight through her. "They've become friends already."

Just like her and Clay. The word had a nice ring to it. But as the warmth of his touch heated, the idea that they'd grown to be friends morphed into something steamier—the fact that they could become lovers again.

She turned to face him, and his splayed fingers trailed away from her back. Their gazes met and locked. Something strong and powerful passed between them, although she'd be darned if she knew what it was. A Colorado memory for sure. A vital connection of some kind. An unbreakable bond?

Before she could possibly give it a name, Clay reached for her face with his right hand and cupped her jaw. His calloused thumb caressed her cheek, singeing her skin and turning her brains to mush.

Before she could decide how to respond to the arousing turmoil he caused her, he placed his left index finger underneath her chin and tilted her face up to his. Her lips parted, and he brushed his mouth across hers.

Unable to help herself, she slipped into his embrace as if she belonged there, as if they'd never been apart, and leaned into him, her breasts pressing against his broad chest. She savored his heady scent—leather, a manly soap and a hint of musk.

He urged her mouth open, and she allowed his tongue to sweep inside and mate with hers until her knees weakened. The sweet, arousing assault intensified until she feared she'd melt into a puddle on the ground if she didn't hold on tight.

As their hands stroked and caressed each other's bodies, a blast of desire surged to her core, creating an empty ache only he could fill.

She'd told herself she wasn't going to make love with him again. Not until they both knew his true identity and could make a decision based on facts rather than lust. But right now, her hormones had taken her common sense hostage, and she wasn't sure about anything anymore.

She might have kissed him until sunrise tomorrow, but he was the first to end it as he slowly drew his lips from hers.

"Damn, Alana." He let out a little whistle and

shook his head. "My memory may have taken a long hike to nowhere, but you'd think I'd remember a kiss like that."

"You don't?" she asked, her voice coming out all soft and wispy.

"I certainly won't forget this one. And I'd give anything to relive that night we met."

So would she.

"I'd ask you to go with me to my bedroom," he added, "but…"

Her heartbeat stammered. "But what?"

He scrubbed a hand over his jaw, then blew out a sigh. "I can see why we made love that night in Colorado. I no doubt found you captivating." He reached up and fingered a strand of her wavy dark hair. "And I'm certainly taken by you now. But something doesn't feel right about falling into a relationship when I don't know who I am."

She could understand that. It went without saying that he might be married or seriously dating someone. Maybe not on the night they met, because he didn't seem like the kind of guy who'd cheat. But a lot could happen in four months.

As if reading her mind, he said, "I can't remember if there's someone else in my life, but I don't think we should complicate things by making love again until I know for sure."

She stepped back, frozen, as if he'd thrown a bucket of ice water on her desire.

"Don't get me wrong," he said. "I want to take you to bed, more than anything right now, except…"

She knew what he meant, and while she was disappointed, it was an honorable decision. So shouldn't she chalk that up as just one more attribute to put on his good-guy list? That is, unless he'd been married when they'd met and he'd taken advantage of her in Colorado.

"Are you okay with waiting?" he asked.

Maybe.

"I hope you understand," he added.

"Yes, of course." She tucked a strand of hair behind her ear. "Don't worry, Clay. I'm sure your memory will come back. It's just a matter of when. And at that time, we can decide if we want our friendship to develop into something more." *That is, unless you need to run home to someone else.*

"Then, that's the plan." He cupped her cheek, then brushed a brotherly kiss on her brow. Only trouble was, she wasn't having sisterly feelings for him. And friendship didn't cut it, either. Because she'd begun to think that Clay just might be everything she'd ever wished for in a man.

Then again, she could be wrong about that. And she had a baby to think about, to protect. She also had to protect herself.

How much more disappointment could her battered heart take?

* * *

After feeding the dogs and making sure they were settled in the barn, Alana retreated to her room. Alone. But her mind hadn't let her sleep. Instead, it kept replaying memories of that night in Colorado, as well as that kiss they'd shared in the yard, creating a never-ending loop. And to make matters worse, the latest blasted kiss had been even better than those she remembered.

After tossing and turning and pounding her fist into her pillow a hundred times trying her best to get comfortable, she'd finally dozed off around two, although she still hadn't gotten any real rest. Just knowing that the gorgeous hunk was only a few steps down the hall, stretched out on the guest bed, all tall and buff and sexy, had her hormones running amok.

No wonder she'd lost her head over him in Colorado. And if he hadn't come to his senses first, she might have done it again last night. He'd barely placed his lips on hers when memories of their lovemaking in his hotel room had exploded in her mind, and she'd been sorely tempted to take him by the hand, lead him into the house and straight to her bedroom.

I can't remember if there's someone else in my life, he'd said, *but I don't think we should complicate things by making love again until I know for sure.*

The truth of that had been staggering, but she'd had to agree. Their chemistry might be off the charts, but that didn't mean anything until they both learned who he really was. Heck, she didn't even know his last name! And try as she might, she couldn't still the little voice at the back of her mind that kept asking, *Is there another woman in his life?*

As all the insecurities that had plagued her over her first twenty years popped up, she batted them down in a game of whack-a-mole, determined to come out a permanent winner.

Finally, around nine o'clock, she got out of bed and took a shower. Now, as she stood in front of the full-length bedroom mirror and tried to zip up her jeans to no avail, she grimaced and gave up.

"That's it," she muttered. So much for leaving the top button undone and hiding her growing girth with a baggy shirt or blouse. The gap in her waistband was going to be too difficult to cover before she knew it. And that meant she couldn't hide it from Clay much longer. She'd have to tell him before he figured it out on his own. At the rate her belly was expanding, she'd better do it soon—like in the next day or so. All she had to do was find the right words to say, gather the courage to say them and then face the consequences.

In the meantime... She blew out a ragged sigh. She'd put off the inevitable for as long as she could. As much as she hated to tap into her limited savings account, she'd have to bite the financial bullet and buy a few more suitable outfits.

But that didn't mean she'd have to venture off to a big city to find a fancy mall or department store. A couple of months ago, while she'd been at the bank in downtown Fairborn, she'd spotted a shop that sold secondhand clothing on the corner of Aspen and Main. The sign over the door read Wear It Again, Sam, which seemed like a clever name for a store selling gently used clothes, but the display in the front window suggested it also offered vintage outfits, which had intrigued her.

So what if she ended up looking like a flower child from the 1960s? Or Cyndi Lauper in the '80s? People might think she had an artsy, eccentric side. That was certainly better than looking as if she was strapped for cash.

What would Clay think of her new style? Not that it really mattered, she supposed. If he was as rich as he'd seemed to be the night they met, then their relationship wouldn't stand the chance of a floating ice cube in a mug of steaming English breakfast tea.

And speaking of breakfast, she'd better eat. Every now and then, she still got a little nauseous if she didn't keep something in her stomach. So she removed her pants, hung them back in the closet and slipped on a pair of stretchy black leggings. Then, after putting on a roomy red flannel shirt that once belonged to her grandfather, she padded down the hall and crossed the small living room. She paused for a moment and studied the worn but cozy sofa, where she and Grandpa had sat many evenings, getting to know each other while enjoying the warm fire on the hearth.

Tears stung the backs of her eyes. How she wished that the *real* Jack McGee was still here, that she could still tap into his trove of memories, his love, his guidance. Maybe he'd suggest the perfect way for her to level with Clay and explain why she'd kept her secret to herself.

She took a deep, fortifying breath, then slowly let it out and headed for the kitchen, the aroma of a hearty breakfast growing stronger with each step she took.

When she reached the open doorway, she found Clay scrambling eggs. He'd already made a pot of coffee and fried five or six crispy strips of bacon.

He must have heard her footsteps, because he turned to her and smiled sheepishly. "I hope you don't mind that I whipped up breakfast this morning."

"No. Not at all." She actually liked seeing him in a domestic setting. It allowed her to imagine him...

No, don't even go there.

What if he actually *did* have a wife or a girl-friend? After all, he appeared to be a good catch. And if that were the case, he was a cad.

The confusion she felt about him made her head spin. And that made her want to hold on to her secret a while longer, even if she shouldn't. And couldn't. But what *was* Clay doing in Fairborn, anyway?

"Katie already fed the boys," he said.

Alana scanned the kitchen, then craned her neck to peer out the window over the sink that looked out into the backyard. "It's awfully quiet. Where *are* the boys?"

"A couple of kids who play on their ball team are in Cub Scouts and encouraged them to join so they could earn badges and go on campouts. Katie took them to check things out and talk to one of the leaders today."

"Cool. That'd be a great experience for them." Alana crossed the room, removed a carton of or-ange juice from the fridge and poured herself a glass.

Clay pulled a couple of plates from the cup-board. "So what have you got planned for today?"

"I'm going into town," she said.

"Oh, yeah? Mind if I go with you? We're running low on alfalfa, and I thought I'd go by the feed store and pick up a few bales. You mentioned having an account there. And since the dog population around here is growing, I better pick up some food for them, too."

The last thing she wanted him to know is what she was up to and why, but she couldn't very well suggest they make two separate trips in the ranch pickup. It had enough miles on the odometer already, and she hardly needed it to break down.

"Sure," she said, "we can ride together. If you don't mind, I'll have you drop me off downtown before you go to the feed store. I have a few errands to run while I'm there, but I don't mind walking. Maybe we can meet at the Mulberry Café for a late-morning snack."

"Sounds like a plan."

Alana headed for the pantry, where she kept her stash of herbal tea, and pulled out a blueberry flavor.

"Just so you know," Clay said. "I'm going to ask around town and see if I can find temporary work. You know, off the books so I don't need to provide an ID."

The comment took her aback, although she wasn't sure why. Did he often do things "off the books"? Then again, he didn't have an ID or even a credit card. And she couldn't very well hold him captive on the ranch.

"I'll still pull my own weight here," he added, "but I've got to earn some money. I don't like being broke."

She didn't figure he did. And she couldn't blame him. If he really *was* the well-heeled attorney he'd said he was, he wouldn't have a care in the world about money. Unlike her—from her humble childhood to her struggles with the ranch today. When she considered the clothing he wore, the way he'd carried himself at the Colorado hotel as well as the pricey tequila he'd been drinking, she had no reason to doubt his economic status.

And that was just one more reason why they'd be a mismatch. The city slicker lawyer and the fledgling rancher. They lived in such different worlds. Chemistry and great sex aside, they didn't have anything in common. And allowing herself even to imagine otherwise was just plain crazy—and a heartbreak ready to happen.

Alana didn't say much on the ride into town, and neither did Clay.

"Here we are," he said, as he pulled up in front of Fairborn Savings and Trust, which was located on the first floor of a two-story, redbrick building.

Alana opened the passenger door, but before climbing out of the vehicle, she turned to the handsome driver who'd begun to look more and more like a cowboy every day. "At the feed store, if you find the parts you're going to need to fix that leaky pump, go ahead and pick them up. Just tell Sam, the owner, to put it on my account."

A somber expression crossed his face, one that was hard for her to decipher. Had a memory popped up in his mind? One that was confusing?

Or maybe disturbing?

"Clay? Are you okay?"

His eye twitched, then he seemed to shake it off—whatever *it* was. "Sure. I'm fine. I'll meet you at the diner."

Once he drove off, Alana turned toward the entrance of the bank. Before reaching for the door, she glanced upstairs where several other businesses were located, one of them the law office of Henry Dahlberg, her grandfather's old high school friend and his personal attorney. Henry was nearing retirement and worked only part-time. He must be there today, though. There was a light on in his office.

Reminding herself that she had things to do before meeting Clay, she entered the bank and withdrew two hundred dollars from her dwindling account. That took care of the first of two errands she had in town.

After slipping the cash into her wallet and stashing it back in her purse, she went outside, turned left and walked three blocks down the street to Wear It Again, Sam, which was housed in a narrow storefront building with pale yellow walls and purple trim.

She stopped in front of the window and studied the display that, this week, featured a blond mannequin dressed in a black turtleneck sweater, gray plaid miniskirt and white go-go boots. An old style portable phonograph, its lid open and a vinyl record on the turntable, sat to the left.

She took a moment to admire both the prop and the typical '60s outfit, even though it wasn't at all what she was looking for. Then she headed to the entrance.

When she opened the purple door, a bell attached to the top of it jingled as she stepped inside. She caught a whiff of a smell similar to that of an antiques shop, mingled with the various scents of clothing that had spent years hanging in closets or packed in boxes, long forgotten in someone's attic.

An older woman, her silver-streaked dark hair styled in a pixie cut, got up from her seat behind the counter. "Good morning. Or should I say good afternoon?" She lifted her forearm to look at the gold bangle watch that hung on her wrist and then approached with a welcoming smile.

"I don't think it's noon yet," Alana said, but it must be getting close.

The woman, who was wearing red lipstick,

gold hoop earrings, a green blouse, a multicol-
ored gypsy skirt and Birkenstock sandals, stood
in front of Alana. "I'm Zoe, the shop owner. Is
there anything in particular I can help you find?"

"A few dresses. Something summery, I guess.
Light and breezy." Alana brushed her hand over
the shirt that hid her belly. "Loose fitting. Maybe
something with an empire waistline."

"Hmm…" Zoe placed an index finger with a
long crimson acrylic nail on her chin, tapping it
as she gave Alana's request some thought. Then
she brightened. "Actually, a woman and her
aunt just stopped by with several boxes of stuff
they want to sell on consignment. The aunt was
around your age, in the sixties, and the clothes
seem to be in good condition. And very boho
chic. I haven't gone through it all yet, but I saw
a couple of dresses that might work. I don't have
them priced or on hangers, but you can still take
a look at them."

"That would be great. Thanks."

As Alana followed the owner through the shop,
Zoe glanced over her shoulder. "Carlene Tipton
finally convinced her aunt to clean out her closet
since Betty Sue was a bit of a hoarder, especially
when it came to her clothes. So I'm looking forward to seeing everything they brought in."

Betty Sue was a spunky woman in her seventies with curly dyed-red hair. Carlene said Betty

had always been a free spirit—and a real character. She'd recently moved in with the Tiptons and spent most of the day at their market, which was only a mile or two away from Rancho Esperanza. It was a godsend to be able to stop in for a few things whenever Alana didn't want to drive all the way into town.

"It'll be interesting to see what she's selling," Alana said, as she entered the back room that was jam-packed with boxes, shoes and clothing. Apparently, Betty Sue wasn't the only one with a tendency to hoard. Probably a boon for Zoe's business!

Zoe stopped beside three cartons, one of which had been opened. "Betty has always been odd, or maybe I should say eccentric. I'd heard she was also wild and rebellious, especially during the '60s. Did you ever see the movie *Grease*? Betty Sue might've been the inspiration for the Rizzo character."

Alana grinned. "I always did love that movie— and the music."

Zoe reached into the open box, pulled out a man's black leather jacket, gave it a shake, then lifted it like a flag. "See? What'd I tell you?"

Alana smiled. "I know what you mean."

Zoe set the jacket aside, then stepped back. "Feel free to rummage through these. If you find something you like, you'll need to launder it before you wear it. Not that it's dirty. It's just that Betty likes to sneak a smoke every now and then." She reached back into the box, pulled out a tie-dyed shirt, held it up to her nose and took a whiff. "Yep. Just what I thought. Menthols."

No surprise there. Alana couldn't help but smile. "Carlene told me Betty also likes to sneak a drink."

"You got that right. Her preference is Jack Daniel's on the rocks with a splash of water, but I don't think she's picky." Zoe backed away from the clothes, giving Alana room to dig through them herself. "Poor Carlene. She sure has her hands full with her aunt, especially since she babysits her two grandkids and also runs the store."

That was true, Alana supposed. But there was something honest and refreshing about Betty, at least from her own perspective.

"The Tiptons think that she has dementia," Zoe added. "And she might."

Alana wasn't so sure about that.

"But don't kid yourself." Zoe lifted her finger and waggled it. "That ol' gal is a lot slyer than some people might think."

Alana had noticed that when Carlene was around, Betty's shoulders slumped and she shuffled when she walked. But she'd also seen her straighten up and move spryly, as if she was on a mission. Like that time she'd been at Callie's baby shower. She'd slipped out the back door, gone to the orchard and returned with a pocket full of ripe cherries.

"Once you find something you like," Zoe said, "we can talk about the price."

Alana thanked her, then began her search. About halfway into the first box, she pulled out a midlength, light blue dress with a delicate lace trim. She held it up and didn't see any reason why it wouldn't fit.

Zoe pointed at the sundress. "There's a tear under the arm. Since I'd have to repair it before laundering it and then putting it on a hanger, I'll sell it to you at a discount. Maybe ten dollars?"

"How about nine?" Alana asked.

Zoe laughed. "A bargain hunter, huh? Sure. Why not?"

Several minutes later, and in a different box, one Carlene hadn't brought in, Alana found a white dress, a denim jacket, a pair of stretch pants and a couple of tops. Then she took her findings to the front of the store, where Zoe tallied the total.

After being paid in cash, Zoe folded the clothes, placed them in a shopping bag and handed them to Alana. "Here you go. I hope to see you again soon."

"Thanks, Zoe. You've got a great shop. I'll be

back." Then she headed to the Mulberry Café, where she and Clay had agreed to meet.

As she neared the downtown eatery, with its blue-and-white awning shading the entry, she spotted Marissa Garcia seated on the oak-slatted, wrought iron bench that sat on the sidewalk to the left of the restaurant's door.

"Hey." Marissa brightened. "What brings you to town?"

Alana lifted the bag that held her new, previously worn garments. "Just doing a little shopping. How about you?"

"Waiting for a friend. We're meeting for lunch, but I arrived early."

"Same here."

Marissa lifted a hand to her brow to shade her eyes from the sun. "When I was leaving your place, after the baby shower, I thought about something else you could do to build up your coffers."

Alana was all ears. Marissa had a real knack for coming up with good business plans. "What's your idea?"

"Have you ever considered offering the ranch as a wedding venue?"

Seriously? "No."

"It's a cool place for an outside event," Marissa said. "And even the name Rancho Esperanza sounds romantic."

"True, but what you're suggesting sounds expensive."

"I'll admit it would take a little work. But I think it's something for you to consider. I noticed that copse of weeping willows behind the barn. They'd make a pretty backdrop if you built a gazebo there."

"It's an idea, I guess." But one like that was too wild to consider now. The only money she could spare was already earmarked for the fence repairs, which Clay said would need to be done sooner rather than later.

And even if that weren't the case, she doubted if anyone would be interested in getting married out there. "Don't you think the ranch is a little too remote and hard to find?"

"It might be now. But I overheard a couple of men talking at the donut shop yesterday. One of them said there's a state highway in the works, and from what I gathered, it's going to be located on the west side of Fairborn. And that means it'll run pretty close to your property."

"Interesting," Alana said. "I hadn't heard a word about it."

"That's because it's pretty hush-hush. But I've always had an interest in business and economics. So whenever I hear things like that, I pay attention."

"So what did you hear?" Alana asked.

"Leon Cunningham, the guy who's running against Ramon for mayor, came into the shop with someone he called Tom, although I didn't recognize the man. And Tom mentioned something about the highway and eminent domain. My ears perked up at that. But then Leon snapped at him and told him he'd better shut up if he knew what was good for him."

"That's weird."

"Yeah, I know. A few weeks ago, in one of my classes, the professor gave a lecture on eminent domain. That's when the government can take private property for public use, although they have to pay you for it."

"Even if I don't want to sell?"

"I think so. That's why I thought you ought to know someone might offer to buy a piece of your property."

So far, the only one who'd shown interest in it was Adam Hastings. Had he heard the rumor, too?

No, that wasn't likely. Why would a man from Texas have any concern over things going on in Montana?

Then again, he'd been so dead set on owning her ranch that he'd offered her more than it was probably worth. He hadn't called in a while so maybe he'd finally gotten her message. Rancho Esperanza *wasn't* for sale.

At least, not to him. But what if the county or state wanted to take it?

Was it possible? Was her property in play for a state highway? If so, that would be terrible. It would change everything she liked about Rancho Esperanza. Its beauty. Its ability to be a safe haven, a true escape.

She was no lawyer and wasn't exactly sure what *eminent domain* meant—or how to fight it—but before she could question Marissa further, footsteps sounded up ahead.

Alana glanced up to see two women walking toward the diner. One of them was Olivia McGee, who had been married to Larry, Grandpa's late brother. Larry and Grandpa had inherited adjoining ranches.

Alana had met Olivia only twice before—once at Grandpa's funeral and again at his attorney's office during the reading of the will.

"Well, I'll be," Olivia said, looking a little too smug for comfort. She looked Alana up and down as if she didn't approve of her coming into town wearing leggings and a red flannel shirt, the hem of which hung to her thighs. "Don't tell me you're still trying to make a go of the Lazy M."

Alana bristled, then recovered. "Actually, things are coming along nicely."

Olivia chuffed. "If I were you, I wouldn't waste any more time on it."

Alana stiffened. What an odd thing for her to say. And a mean one. "My time isn't your concern."

"No? Well, we'll see about that." Olivia nudged her companion. "Come on. Let's find a table where we can chat."

Olivia's friend, who looked vaguely familiar, opened the diner door, and the two of them entered.

"What was that all about?" Marissa asked.

"I'll be darned if I know. That was my grandfather's sister-in-law. She was polite—the few times I saw her before. But not today."

"Is she mad at you?"

"She sure seems to be. But I have no idea why."

"What about her friend?" Marissa asked. "Do you know her?"

"She looks familiar, but I'm not sure where we met."

"I don't know her name," Marissa said, "but I heard she works part-time for an attorney. She comes into the donut shop on Thursday mornings and always buys the same thing—a cinnamon twist and a cup of coffee to go. She told me it was for her boss."

Oh. So that's who the woman was—and why she looked vaguely familiar. She worked a couple mornings a week at Henry's law office.

At the rattling engine sound of an approaching vehicle, Alana glanced up and spotted the ranch pickup coming down the street, its bed loaded down with bales of hay.

She'd told Clay to meet her here to have something to eat, but with snarky Olivia inside, Alana no longer had an appetite.

"My ride's here," she told Marissa. "I'll give you a call later and we can talk more."

Just as Clay was pulling into a parking space, Alana strode toward the pickup and opened the passenger door before Clay shut off the ignition.

"Is something wrong?" he asked.

"No. I just need to get home."

He studied her for a moment with a quizzical look, then he checked the rearview mirror, backed up and headed down the street.

If he suspected she'd been lying when she'd told him nothing was wrong, he didn't say.

Thank goodness for that. Because something was definitely not right. She just didn't know what.

Chapter Eight

From the moment Clay spotted Alana in front of the diner, he knew something was wrong. He could read it in her pretty face, see it in the crease in her brow, the flush on her cheeks, the tension around her lips.

His gut clenched at the thought of her dealing with anything unsettling or unpleasant. And since she'd been looking forward to having a sweet treat at the Mulberry Café, something had caused her to skip it completely.

"What happened?" he asked.

"Nothing."

It didn't take a mind reader to see that she wasn't telling him the truth and that she didn't want to talk about it. Certainly not now. And maybe not ever. So he kept his thoughts to himself, turned the old pickup onto the main drag and headed back to the ranch.

Every now and then, he stole a peek at her profile, hoping to see that her mood had lightened, that she'd decided whatever had been bothering her was no longer worth her concern. But worry still marred her brow.

He wished that she'd confide in him and let him carry some of the burden for her, but that wasn't happening. He supposed he couldn't blame her for keeping it to herself. After all, who was he? Just some guy she'd met only once at a cattle symposium. She'd said she'd considered him a friend, but they hadn't met again for four months. So in actuality, he was a virtual stranger who'd stumbled onto her property, battered and bruised. And memory impaired to boot.

She'd taken care of him. And she hadn't needed to. So she felt something for him. Had their lovemaking created a bond? He suspected it had.

Over the past couple of days, he'd experienced a few disjointed memories, visions that popped up briefly. But they hadn't been much help. Instead of allowing him to tap into his past, they'd left him uneasy, and he wasn't sure why.

He was convinced he'd been the victim of a

crime. But what if he was wrong? What if he'd deserved the beating he'd received?

He wished he knew. But what he did know— he glanced across the seat at the woman who'd taken him in, and warmth melted in his chest like a slather of soft butter on a hot biscuit—what he'd come to believe, was that he, like Katie, Jesse and Mark, had found something special there, a haven of sorts. And that realization left him feeling appreciative as well as protective of Alana.

Once they'd gotten a few miles outside town, he decided to give her something else to think about, something that might ease her load. "I got a job. It's only part-time, but it'll give me some cash."

At that, she turned to him. "Doing what?"

"Helping Sam at the feed store in the mornings. Manny, the college student who works for him, had a death in the family, so Sam needs some immediate help."

"I'm sorry to hear that about Manny. Sam has been having a few health issues himself, which is why he hired Manny in the first place. I'm glad you can help him for a while."

Clay wasn't afraid of hard work. And the position certainly would make his life a little easier while he was upstream without a paddle. Hell, each time he reached into his pocket and came up empty—no credit card, no cash, no freakin'

ID—he had the urge to run home. Only trouble was, he had no idea where home was.

They'd driven just about a mile or two farther when Alana cut a glance at him. "Do you know anything about eminent domain?"

The question took him aback, but mostly because he realized he knew quite a bit about the subject. "That's when a government entity or one of its agents wants to convert private property for public use."

"They can just take it?" Her voice shook, and her brow furrowed as her eyes locked on him.

"Yes, they can. But per the Fifth Amendment, they can only exercise that power if they provide just compensation to the property owner." He gazed at the road ahead, then slid another glance her way and caught her studying him intently. Why was she asking him about this out of the clear blue sky? And why the worried expression?

"Seems to me like you know a lot about the law," she said. "I guess you really *are* an attorney."

Maybe so. But something niggled at him… Something else he ought to know. Something that was locked up with all the other crap he couldn't remember.

Property.

Land acquisitions.

A state highway.

A male voice reverberating through the room. *I'm not* asking *you to give it a try, Clayton. I'm telling you to* close *the deal.*

Clay chewed on the sudden awareness, on the brief memory, hoping he could stir up a bit more from those dark, clouded corners in his mind. Who was the man? Where was the room?

A faint recollection seemed just within reach. The scent of a fine Kentucky bourbon and the clinking of ice cubes in a crystal glass. An open legal brief resting on a massive, solid oak desk. An antique clock on the wall, counting out the seconds with each ticktock.

A built-in bookcase filled with law books. A window providing a view of a couple of horses grazing in a pasture.

The edges of the full memory floated in the mist, but the vision stalled, and try as he might, he couldn't stir up anything else—other than the sense that he hadn't been too keen on the assignment.

He supposed he ought to be happy that things were coming back to him, even if it was only at a snail's pace. But instead, it frustrated the hell out of him, and he squeezed the steering wheel until his knuckles turned white.

Up ahead, he spotted the yellow-and-green mailbox that was perched next to the road leading into Rancho Esperanza and flipped on the turn signal.

He cut another glance at Alana. "Why'd you want to know about eminent domain?"

When he caught her eye, her lips parted as if she was about to explain. Then she shrugged. "No reason. Not really. Just curious."

He couldn't help but doubt her response. Not when he'd seen the concern in her eyes. Besides, topics like that didn't come out of nowhere. But he couldn't very well expect her to trust him with her troubles, assuming she had some. And he really had no right to pry.

As he pulled up into the front yard, two of the dogs dashed out of the barn barking at the pickup, wagging their tails. Rascal, the Queensland Heeler, and Licorice. But where was Chewie?

Chasing a squirrel or pestering the chickens, he supposed.

As Clay and Alana climbed out of the pickup, Mark and Jesse rushed out the back door.

"Guess what?" Jesse called out. "Chewie had her puppies!"

"Four of them!" his older brother added. "And one of them looks a lot like Rascal."

At the boys' joyful news, Alana's mood shifted, and she finally broke into a grin, apparently shedding her worries.

The relief that swept through him was short-lived as a growing sense of uneasiness settled over him.

State highways. Eminent domain.

I'm not asking *you to give it a try, Clayton. I'm telling you to* close *the deal.*

Who'd issued the order? And why?

As the kids and Alana hurried to see the new puppies in the outbuilding, where Katie and the boys had created their separate quarters, Clay remained rooted in the yard, trying to make sense of it all.

His head started to ache, and he rubbed his temples.

Why was he here? Why had he left Texas, if that's where he actually lived? What was he doing in Montana? Had he merely come to look up an old lover he'd apparently met only once? Or had there been more to it than that?

No. There wasn't. He now remembered enough of the night they'd met that he had something to hang on to.

He ticked off the sequence of events again to be sure. He and Alana had met in a Colorado bar and hit it off immediately. They'd made love that night, and she'd slipped away before they could make plans to see each other again. And it had taken him four months to find her.

He had no idea how his head injury had come

about, but even in a befuddled state, he'd found his way to Alana—and to Rancho Esperanza.

That scenario, more than anything else, made the most sense. So as far as he was concerned, that'd be his story, and he was sticking to it.

He kicked a rock out of his way as he headed toward the barn to check on Bailey, the mare about to foal. He slowed. Suddenly, the memory of that male voice plus the vision of an office struck him a whole different way, especially when he considered that he knew a hell of a lot about law and real estate.

Had he really come to Montana in an attempt to find Alana because he'd longed to see her again?

And why, when any private investigator worth his salt could have found her in short order, had it taken him four long months?

Two days later, after Clay had gone to work at the feed store and Katie had taken the boys to the library in town to participate in a children's summer reading program, Alana went into the ranch office and began paying the regular monthly bills.

She'd barely signed her name on a check to the power company when the dogs began to bark, alerting her that someone had arrived at the ranch. So she got up from her seat and went to see who it was.

Just as she reached the living room, the screen squeaked open and a hard *knock-knock-knock* sounded.

"I'm coming," she called out.

When she opened the door, she found an unfamiliar middle-aged man wearing a tie and sports jacket standing on the porch. He held some paperwork in his hand.

Alana offered up a smile, but he didn't return it.

All right, then.

"Can I help you?" she asked.

"Are you Alana Perez?"

At his serious tone, her smile faded. "Yes, that's me."

He handed her the papers. "You've been served."

Stunned, she remained in the doorway until he returned to the yard, climbed into a nondescript white sedan and drove away. Then she looked over the legal document he'd given her.

Her jaw dropped, and her heart pounded out a scream in a weird, cardiac Morse code. *"Seriously?"* Olivia McGee was contesting Grandpa's will and challenging Alana's inheritance?

This couldn't be happening. No way.

Alana closed the door, sequestering herself in

the small, cozy living room that, in months past, had provided her with peace but didn't offer her any right now.

She made her way to the brown tweed sofa and plopped down, sinking into the worn, frayed cushions she used to find comfortable. Today, they felt only cold, hard and unyielding. She continued to read the complaint.

Olivia claimed that Alana had taken advantage of a sick and lonely old man, that she'd encouraged him to change his will while he was heavily sedated on pain medication and to leave his entire estate to her.

Her hands trembled as she tried to make sense of it all. Not the fact that the will was being contested. That was obvious. But why now, after more than six months had passed? Weren't there time limits on this kind of thing?

She needed help. And advice. She got up and returned to the office. She searched through Grandpa's Rolodex for Henry's number. He was the one who'd drawn up the will. He'd know what to do. She reached for the telephone receiver, but before she could remove it from the cradle, she froze.

Olivia had been with the woman who worked for Henry. Was Grandpa's attorney involved?

Instead, she reached for her cell phone, which rested on the scarred dark pine desk. She looked through her contact list and then dialed Ramon Cruz, Callie's husband. The man was incredibly busy, but she knew if he had a moment to spare he'd give her wise counsel—and, hopefully, some sound advice.

"Hey," Ramon said. "How's it going?"

"Not so good. I'm sorry to bother you, but I've got a big problem. A legal one, and I didn't know who else to call."

"What's up?"

"I've just been served papers." She gave him the details.

Ramon let out a sigh. "That's unfortunate. Give me some time. I'll try to get more information. Then we can come up with a solid game plan."

We. She liked the sound of that.

After disconnecting, Alana began to pace the office floor. Time seemed to stand still as one ticktock stretched into another.

Finally, nearly thirty minutes later, Ramon called back.

"What'd you find out?" she asked.

"Olivia's Kalispell attorney not only backs up Olivia's claims that you hoodwinked your grandfather and stole property that had been previously willed to her and her late husband, but he also believes Jack's attorney should have retired from practice years ago."

"That's a downright lie. And for what it's worth, Grandpa was completely lucid at the time. He'd even refused pain medication until the day before he died because he wanted to spend as much quality time with me as he could. You can even ask Henry."

"I'm afraid talking to him won't be much help. And his testimony could be even more damaging. It's a known fact around town that he's been having some memory issues. And lately, it's gotten worse. He retired last month."

Alana's shoulders slumped, and she leaned against the wall. Henry Dahlberg had been her sole witness. Now what?

"For what it's worth," Ramon added, "it seems that Olivia recently sold her ranch. The escrow should close within the next week or so."

A shiver of suspicion slithered up and down Alana's spine. There was only one man intent upon snatching up ranches in the area. "Don't tell me. A man named Adam Hastings bought it."

"That's what I heard. And confidentially, I heard she got more than it's worth."

"Then, why is she going after my property?"

Ramon didn't answer right away, then he said, "Honestly, none of this passes the smell test. I'll poke around and see if I can find out anything else."

"Thank you. Your advice?"

"Lawyer up."

Alana sank to the couch and pressed her hands over her swelling belly. As reality settled over her, she realized she was in for a costly and lengthy legal battle.

And one she just might lose.

For a forty-five-year-old man who stood about six foot six and was built like an NFL offensive lineman, Sam Willis, the owner of Fairborn Feed and Grain, wasn't the least bit intimidating. Surprisingly, he was a soft-spoken, gentle giant. A scraggly beard, mostly in need of a trim, suggested he was a little rough around the edges, but a ready smile that put a sparkle in his eyes argued otherwise.

From what Clay had heard from several of the locals who patronized the feed store, Sam was also honest. "He's as generous as the good Lord made 'em," one older gentleman claimed. And it hadn't taken long for him to agree on all accounts.

On Thursday morning, Clay arrived early, about fifteen minutes before Sam opened for the day, a habit he'd acquired since his first day working at the busy feed store.

"Good morning," Clay said, as Sam unlocked the front door and let him inside.

Sam gave a tired sigh and muttered, "G' mornin'."

Clay paused in the doorway and studied his slump-shouldered boss. "You okay?"

Sam grimaced as he stroked his stomach. "Yeah. Just got a bellyache. That's all. Started last night." He pointed to the rear of the store. "Would you mind bringing in a couple sacks of chicken feed up front? The display stack is getting low."

"Sure." After completing the task, Clay glanced at the clock near the register, where Sam was adding coins into the till. "Is Manny coming in today?"

"He said he was, although I told him he didn't have to. His uncle's funeral was yesterday, and I think he should stick close to home." Sam chuffed, then slowly shook his head. "I like that kid. He's a hard worker, smart and responsible. He's been a real godsend to me. But he has to help his aunt run the ranch until she can hire a foreman."

"I can give you as much help as you need," Clay said. "At least, for the time being."

"Thanks. I appreciate that."

After several customers had come in and then checked out, Manny finally came dragging in.

"Sorry I'm late," he told Sam. "My car wouldn't

start, and my aunt and I had to feed the horses before she could give me a ride."

Other than Manny getting a late start, the morning began as usual, with customers coming in and out. But by eleven o'clock, the day seemed to shift into one that was anything but typical. The pain in Sam's gut had clearly gotten worse.

"Maybe you ought to see a doctor," Clay told him.

Sam lifted the brim of a brown-and-gold Wyoming Cowboys baseball cap he always wore and scrubbed a big, beefy hand over his bald head. After replacing the cap and adjusting it, he stroked his scraggly beard. "Nah. I just took some antacids. It'll go away pretty soon."

But it didn't go away, and by noon, Sam was nearly doubled over in pain. Still, the tough guy continued to work, this time helping a local rancher load several sacks of grain in the bed of a dual-wheeled pickup.

Before Sam could lift another fifty-pound bag, Clay reached for his arm and stopped him. "Put that down. I'll get it."

"No need. I can do it."

"This is crazy, Sam. Call your wife and have her drive you to the hospital. Manny and I'll hold down the fort while you're gone."

"It's probably something I ate," the stubborn man said.

Clay had his doubts. Before he could object, a memory crept into his consciousness.

A summer day. The smell of alfalfa growing in the field. The whinny of horses out in the pasture.

A man walking out to a big white barn, with three boys tagging along behind him.

The smallest kid, barely twelve or thirteen, was bringing up the rear, his face contorted. *Dad, I hate to complain. But I got a real bad stomachache.*

His father didn't slow down. Nor did he look back. He just continued toward the barn. *I've been trying to cut you some slack, Clayton. I know you're still grieving, but you need to shake it off. And toughen up. We've got work to do.*

How do you expect him to get tough? the older of the two other boys said. *He'd rather be wearing baggy pants and playin' around at the skate park in Dallas.*

At that, both of the teenage boys—Clay's half brothers, he was sure of it—snickered.

But no one was laughing when the paramedics placed Clay on a gurney and rushed him to the hospital.

They'd been at a ranch in Texas, although he wasn't sure in which part it was actually located. All he knew for certain was that his appendix had burst sometime that day and he'd spent nearly a week in the hospital.

His heart stopped as he realized something: it was the same hospital where his mom had died.

"Oh, wow." As the pieces of a puzzling memory began to fall in place, Clay's feet froze like two big blocks of ice on the feed store floor. His mother had died. An accidental prescription-drug overdose.

Oh, crap. And Clay had been the one to find her. The scene roared back to him like punches to the gut. The ambulance. He'd ridden in it, too. Flashing lights. The siren screaming out into the night.

DOA. DOA!

He'd clutched the note she'd left on the nightstand that had indicated it hadn't been an accident at all. After reading it, he'd shoved it into his pocket—a dark family secret from that day on.

I'm sorry, honey. I can't do this anymore. And I'm no good to you like this. Call your daddy. He'll take care of everything.

After talking to a social worker at the hospital, who'd tried to make things better but hadn't, he'd made the call to his father, a man he'd seen sparingly. He couldn't remember a thing that woman had said to him, but he remembered every red-hot word he'd cried into the pay phone's receiver. *It's all your fault, you son of a bitch. Right after she lost the baby, you left her.* Again! *And it broke her heart and messed her up. That's why she stayed in bed all the time with the curtains closed.*

I'm coming to get you, Clayton. You're going to come live with me and your older brothers on the ranch.

And he had. Right? Hadn't he?

The rest faded back into the shadowy holes of his memory, which wasn't much more than a block of Swiss cheese.

He wished the rest of it would come back to him, but the memory seemed to freeze up like a frame in a damaged DVD.

Clay sucked in a deep breath, then approached his boss. "Sam, I'm no doctor, but the pain is clearly getting worse. You need to have it checked out."

Sam grimaced, then shook his head. "I'm not going to close the store early for something that's bound to pass."

"If it's appendicitis and you wait too long, you could end up closing the store for weeks. Don't ask me how I know. I just do."

An hour later, Sam finally relented. After leaving Manny to hold down the fort, he climbed into the passenger seat of his late-model Dodge Ram pickup. Clay got behind the wheel, then he drove to the hospital, where Sam's wife would meet them.

Twenty minutes later, with Sam slumped against the passenger window, Clay turned into the driveway and followed the signs pointing to the emergency department. A dark sense of foreboding smacked him, much like the one he'd experienced when he'd taken Alana to check on Callie.

His gut twisted into a knot, and he clutched the steering wheel with cold, clammy hands.

Again, he was struck with the same, childlike conclusion. Bad things happened at hospitals. People died. Kids were left alone and confused... Scared. Heartbroken.

And dads didn't always come through like they should.

Only trouble was, he couldn't quite get a bead on his father's face. Or his mother's. But he was certain of one thing, even if he couldn't explain just how he knew it—his parents had never been married. They'd broken up right after he was born, and his dad hadn't come around very much. Then his parents started seeing each other again.

He blew out a frustrated sigh. He'd give anything to have his memory come back all at once, but that didn't appear to be happening. At least, not anytime soon.

As he stopped in front of the emergency entrance, he shut off the engine. "Wait here, Sam. I'll get a wheelchair."

Before he could enter the emergency department and ask for one, the automatic door swung open, and a woman rushed out, worry and concern stretched across her face. She smacked her hand against the truck's window. "Sam, I swear you're the most stubborn man I've ever met. I told you to stay home today."

Sam grimaced. "The boss doesn't call in sick, honey."

Mrs. Willis turned to Clay. "Thank you for bringing him here. I'll take over now."

"All right. I'll drive the truck back. The keys will be in Sam's desk."

He watched the hospital staff take over, put Sam in a wheelchair and parade inside. Then Clay climbed behind the wheel and headed to the feed store, hoping Sam would be okay.

As he drove, he tried to make better sense of his feelings and the memories he'd just experienced, as brief and fleeting as they'd been.

Then another memory wormed its way to the surface.

I've got bad news, a doctor had said. *Your mom's going to be okay in time, but the baby didn't make it. We had to sedate her, so we're going to keep her overnight. Do you have anyone you can call? Someone who can take you home and stay with you?*

He must have called someone, although he had no idea who. Unfortunately, he hadn't been able to dig up any more than that.

Damn. Why couldn't he remember the rest?

By the time he returned to the feed store, he'd done his best to put it behind him. There was no need to beat himself up about it. Besides, he needed to get to work.

A couple of hours later, his cell phone rang. It was Sam.

"What'd the doctor say?" Clay asked.

"I got a dad-blasted bleeding ulcer. Can you believe that? And they want to keep me overnight. Hell, I can't do that. I've got a store to run."

"Between Manny and me, we can keep things going until you're back. Just follow the doctor's orders and get well."

"But I told Manny he could have a few days off," Sam said. "His aunt has a large spread to run, and she can't do it on her own. She and her husband damn near raised him. He ought to spend some time at home with her."

"It might help if he kept busy. Besides, the kid thinks the world of you."

Sam didn't respond at first, then he sighed. "I guess you're right. But give him whatever time he needs to help her out. He's a good kid, he'll make it up as he's able to."

It was, Clay supposed, difficult for some men to share their feelings. Was he one of them? No, that couldn't be. He had come here to Montana, looking for Alana to tell her...what? *I love you?* That didn't seem quite right, either.

Why was it so damned easy for him to remember some of the crappy times in his life?

Surely he'd had some good times, too.

Tamping down his frustration, Clay got busy helping customers and loading vehicles with their supplies until finally, at six o'clock, he and Manny closed up the feed store and locked the door.

Then Clay drove to the ranch where Manny lived with his aunt.

"Thanks," Manny said, as he climbed out of the passenger seat of the pickup.

"Take all the time you need in the morning. I can open the store on my own."

"You got it."

As Manny walked toward the white, two-story clapboard house, Clay pulled back onto the road and drove home.

No, not *home*. Back to the ranch.

And back to Alana.

For the first time all day, warmth filled his chest and a smile stretched across his face.

Rancho Esperanza might be a temporary place for him to stay, but damn. Wherever he really lived, be it a rustic mountain cabin, a high-rise loft in the city or a sprawling estate in the foothills, he had reason to believe he'd never really looked forward to going home.

Not like he did tonight.

Chapter Nine

Alana expected Clay to get off around noon and head back to the ranch for lunch, just like he'd done the past few days. Assuming they'd eat together again today, she made two turkey sandwiches, cut a couple wedges of cheddar cheese and sliced an apple.

When he hadn't shown up by two, she covered his plate with plastic wrap, placed it in the fridge and then ate by herself.

For the rest of the afternoon, she kept busy by giving the kitchen a thorough cleaning, peeling carrots and potatoes and fixing a pot roast for dinner. But with each passing hour, she'd grown more and more worried about him.

If he'd had a cell phone, she would have called or sent him a text earlier. She'd even thought about calling the feed store and asking Sam if Clay had mentioned anything about having to run some errands in town, but she'd opted not to do that. The last thing in the world she wanted to do was to give Clay a reason to believe that she was pushing boundaries, even if they hadn't yet established any. So she'd decided against that, too. But now, as the six o'clock hour approached, Clay still hadn't come home.

Uneasy, Alana made a tossed salad, using cucumbers and tomatoes from the garden, and placed the bowl on the table. Then she returned to the stove, where the roast was cooking in a Dutch oven. With a frayed red pot holder, she lifted the lid to check the meat. Nicely browned and juicy, it certainly looked like it was done. And it smelled delicious.

She reached into the drawer, pulled out a fork and poked it into the biggest carrot. Yes. Dinner was ready.

Katie and the boys would be coming home any minute, but where was Clay? She shut off the flame under the pot and then glanced at the clock yet again. It was now well after six. The feed store had closed fifteen minutes ago.

Something must have happened. Something bad, like a car accident. Or maybe Clay had suffered some kind of relapse, and his amnesia had gotten worse. What if he'd made a wrong turn and gotten lost?

Then again, he could've had engine trouble. That old pickup wasn't very dependable. If it broke down along the road, Clay wouldn't have any way to contact her.

Okay, Alana. Stop already. You're not his nanny or mother. Back off. It's not like we have a commitment.

Besides, he wasn't an invalid or a kid. He was a grown man, and his whereabouts weren't any of her business.

That might be true, but tell that to her troubled heart. She checked the time once more. The minute hand was moving toward the half hour.

Okay, so Clay didn't need a caretaker. But over a short period of time, he and Alana had become friends. And friends cared about each other, checked in on them, made sure they were doing okay.

So, that being the case, Alana had every right to be concerned about his safety and well-being. She stole another peek at the clock. Maybe there'd been a problem at the feed store, and he had to work late. That made sense.

So even if it was after closing time, someone might still be there and could answer the phone. What would it hurt to call?

Not a blasted thing. She strode across the kitchen, snatched her cell from its charger and, after checking the list of commonly dialed numbers Grandpa had tacked to the wall, she called the feed store.

No answer.

Darn it. She should have phoned sooner.

Just as she was about to call Katie and ask to borrow her car, the familiar rumble of the old truck's engine sounded in the side yard.

She let out a weary sigh and muttered, "Thank goodness."

Moments later, the back door squeaked open. It took every ounce of her self-control not to hurry to the service porch to greet him, to ask where he'd been and why he was late. Instead, she pretended as if she hadn't given his tardiness any thought at all.

"I'm back," Clay called out.

"Oh, good. Dinner's almost ready."

"It smells great," he said. "Katie and the boys just got home. She's getting something out of her trunk, but the boys ran to the barn."

"They're probably checking on the horses."

"That's my guess," Clay said. "Do I have time to take a shower before dinner?"

"Sure. But…" Unable to help herself, Alana placed her hands on her hips and asked, "Where've you been? I was getting worried."

Oh, crap. She hadn't meant to blurt that out. Would he think she was getting too attached? Would he accuse her of smothering him, the way her ex-boyfriend Bradley once had?

Damn, Alana. I don't have to account to you for every minute I'm away. Can't a guy have a weekend to himself?

A look of surprise crossed his face. "I'm sorry," he said, his tone contrite. "I should've called to let you know I had to work late. Sam was having some health issues and had to cut out early, so Manny and I took over for him. It turns out he has a bleeding ulcer. Then we got slammed with customers this afternoon. I'm sorry if I made you worry."

"I'm just glad you're okay," she said. "But what about Sam? My grandfather said he never takes a day off. That can't be good for him."

"He's in the hospital, but they'll probably release him soon. In the meantime, I told him I'd cover for him."

"I'm sure he was relieved to hear that."

"So was his wife. I talked to her right before closing time. The doctor thinks Sam has been under too much stress, and that he ought to take some time off. She's hopeful that he'll agree to a vacation, although she admitted he can be stubborn at times."

"I'm glad you're able to help out," Alana said.

Not that she was happy Clay would be gone more. But it was nice to know that Sam and his wife thought he was dependable, responsible and trustworthy.

Her gaze locked on his, and the room seemed to close in on them. He'd charmed her back in Colorado when he'd been dressed in a designer sports jacket, but there was something more appealing about him now. Even the smell of dust and straw couldn't drown out his usual, alluring scent of soap and man.

But she'd be darned if she was going to fawn over him like a lovesick adolescent. So she tore her eyes away from him, turned her back and reached for the pot holder she'd left on the counter near the stove.

"I'll put dinner on the table," she said. "But you have time for a quick shower."

"Good. I'd like that. I won't be long."

As he left the room, she tried not to think about him in the bathroom, removing his shirt, slipping out of his pants. Standing under the spray of warm water, running a bar of soap over his slick skin.

Oh, for Pete's sake. Get a grip, girl.

Instead of imagining herself climbing into the shower with him, she reminded herself she had bigger problems than getting lathered up with her former lover. There was a court date looming on the horizon, and she stood to lose the ranch.

She let out a sigh as she removed the carrots and potatoes from the Dutch oven. She'd been disappointed many times in life and had learned how to adapt to a loss, but never one like this. Rancho Esperanza had become a haven, not only for her and the stray dogs she'd rescued but for so many others. What would happen to Katie and the boys if Alana lost the ranch? Living rent-free allowed the young woman to remain in college while she raised her young brothers.

Earlier this morning, at Ramon's suggestion, she'd called an attorney in Kalispell. The woman had a great reputation, had her own practice and didn't work in the same firm as the guy Olivia had hired. But Alana couldn't get an appointment until Monday afternoon, which seemed like a long time away.

If Clay actually was an attorney, like he'd claimed to be when they'd met, he might be able to put her heart and mind at ease. He certainly seemed to understand eminent domain.

Could he offer her legal advice? She was sorely tempted to share her dilemma, but the doctor had told her not to force him to remember, and she hated to put any additional pressure on him.

Besides, if he finally remembered who he was,

he'd undoubtedly return to Texas and to the life he'd had there.

And if truth be told, Alana wasn't ready to see him go.

Clay would have preferred to stand under the spray of hot water for hours, but he'd promised to take a quick shower, and he was a man of his word. He paused as that thought took hold. He had integrity. That was good to know. Especially when he'd been told to close a deal of some kind that he sensed had left him a little uneasy.

When he returned to the kitchen, he found Katie setting the table and Alana slicing a big, juicy roast. Before he could ask if there was something he could do to help, the back door squeaked open and one of the boys rushed inside.

"I think you'd better come quick," Jesse said. "There's something wrong with one of the horses. I mean Bailey. She's acting really weird."

"What's she doing?" Clay asked.

"She keeps bumping into the rails of her stall. And then she lies down in the straw. But she gets right back up again. It's like she can't decide what she wants to do. I think she's sick."

Clay pushed his chair way from the table. "I'll go check on her. She's probably getting ready to foal."

Alana got to her feet, too. "I'll go with you. I've never seen a colt be born."

"It's pretty cool," Clay said. He knew that was true, although he couldn't actually recall a specific memory of him seeing a mare foal. But if he'd lived on a ranch, as he'd come to believe, he probably had.

Moments later, Clay and Alana followed Jesse into the barn and back to Bailey's wooden stall. Mark stood just outside the gate, flanked by Rascal and Licorice and watching the chestnut mare shift her weight from side to side and paw at the straw on the ground, stirring up dust.

"Boys," Clay said, "why don't you put the dogs in the house. I don't want them to make the mare nervous."

"I'll do it," Jesse said. "But that'll probably make them sad. They already feel jealous that Chewie and her puppies get to stay with us."

Alana tugged on Clay's shirtsleeve, worry etched upon her face, her eyes seeking his for reassurance. "Is she okay? I mean, I've studied what happens when horses give birth and I've watched a few YouTube videos. But dang. It's different in reality. Is this normal?"

"Yes. Looks like she's in the first stage of labor."

"According to what I've read," Alana said, "this could take some time."

"It can take hours." Again, he wasn't sure how he knew that. He just did. It seemed reasonable to assume he'd have firsthand knowledge, even if he'd been a "city boy" until he was twelve or thirteen.

Alana tugged at his shirtsleeve again, only this time her fingers lingered on his arm. "I don't want to take any chances. Maybe we should call the vet." Her pretty green eyes, framed with thick, dark lashes, locked on his. She was relying on him. Trusting him. "What do you think?"

"I don't think that's necessary." At least, not yet.

"Should we leave her alone?" Alana asked. "I mean, I'd rather not. I want to stay here as long as it takes, but I don't want to bother her."

"Mares usually prefer to be alone when they foal, but it might be okay if you're nearby, as long as you stay out of the way."

"Can we wait with you guys?" Mark asked.

Before Clay could answer, Katie approached and placed her hand on her brother's small shoulder. "Dinner's on the table, boys. It's time to eat. We need to be at Callie's house before seven."

"Aw, man." Jesse turned a frown on his big sister. "I forgot about that. Do we have to?"

Katie stroked the younger boy's hair, then gave it an affectionate tousle. "Coach Ramon asked us to keep Callie company while he's at that town council meeting because he doesn't want her to be by herself. And he said he'd have everything we need to make ice-cream sundaes."

"I don't think you'll miss anything," Clay told the boys. "Bailey probably won't have her baby until morning. Besides, you made a commitment to your coach. And he's depending on you to follow through with it."

"Yeah," Mark said. "He's right. Come on, dude. We gotta go."

As the boys trudged behind their big sister on their way back to the house, Clay watched them go. It was nice to see such connection between the brothers.

The smile that had begun to tug at his lips faded as a memory rose up.

"Clay-dough," Artie said, as he peered into the rearview mirror, "I left my sunglasses down at the lake where we were fishing. Go get 'em for me."

Artie was always leaving things someplace— his keys, his homework, his hat.

"How come I gotta go get 'em?" Clay asked.

"'Cause that's about all you're good for. Just do it, Doughboy."

Clay might have spouted off with an insult or a dumb nickname of his own, but he'd been glad when his brothers had included him for a change, even if he didn't like fishing and had to take a boatload of crap off them. So he climbed out of the backseat of Artie's Jeep and jogged toward the water's edge.

He'd only gotten ten yards away when he heard the engine start up and the tires kick up gravel as the vehicle spun around.

"Clay-dough," Phil hollered out the window. "Have a nice walk home."

It had been a ten-mile walk, and by the time he'd gotten home, dinner was over and he had a couple of blisters on both feet. But he hadn't complained. Or snitched. That would have only made things worse.

As the vision dimmed, revealing little more of that evening, Clay wondered if things had ever gotten any better between him and his brothers. It was impossible to say, so he shook it off. Then he leaned against the stall railing and studied the laboring mare.

"How's she doing?" Alana asked. "I mean, do you see any reason for us to be concerned?"

"No, but why don't you go back in the house and eat with everyone else. I'll stay close by and keep an eye on things out here."

"I'm not going anywhere, Clay. My grandpa pinned his hopes of turning this ranch around on Bailey and that colt. And they're my hope now. So I'm going to stay out here as long as it takes.

And if something goes wrong, I'll have the vet on speed dial."

Her spunk surprised him. In a good way. Unable to help himself, he tossed her a flirtatious smile. "Then, it looks like we'll both be spending the night in the barn."

Her lips parted, and she shot a quizzical look his way. "You're going to stay out here with me?"

He shrugged. "Sure. Why not? I was a Boy Scout once. It might be fun."

"But what about work? Don't you have to open the feed store tomorrow morning?"

"I can get by without sleep." Hell, he'd done it enough times when he'd been at Oklahoma State University and then again in law school.

Well, how about that. The past was slowly coming back to him.

"Okay, then." Alana took a step toward the door. "I'll go inside and get us some blankets. The barn can get cold and drafty at night."

As she turned away and headed back to the house, Clay couldn't help but smile. Camping out with the Scouts was a lot of fun—and clearly another youthful experience that battled itself to the front of his mind—but telling ghost stories to a bunch of guys who didn't think bathing and overnighters went hand in hand couldn't hold a candle to spending the night out here with Alana.

Five minutes later, she returned with two pillows and a couple of blankets. But she wasn't the only one to come back into the barn. Katie came next, holding two sturdy paper plates loaded down with a hearty meal, while Jesse juggled two glasses, each one holding a set of plastic-ware wrapped in a napkin. Mark brought up the rear with a thermos and a worn yellow tablecloth.

"We brung dinner and beds for you guys," Jesse said.

"Brought," his sister corrected.

Alana nodded at the east wall, where an old desk and chair sat. "Clay, would you mind pulling that out for us? We can use it as a table. There's also another chair next to the ladder that's leaning against the hayloft."

"Talk about five-star service." Clay chuckled as he complied with her request.

Alana set the bedding, two blankets and a couple of pillows on a bale of straw. Then she took the faded yellow tablecloth from Mark and covered the desk. "I figured we'd both eat out here. And since we could be staying the night, we may as well be as comfortable as possible."

The guest bed where Clay slept was warm and comfortable. But spending the evening with Alana in a drafty, dusty, straw-littered barn was going to be an interesting experience. Not that either of them would get much sleep once the night air began to infiltrate the gaps in the wood-slatted walls and the mare's labor progressed.

"Alana," Katie said, "I'll clean up before we leave. Ramon said that he felt okay leaving Callie alone for a few minutes. So the boys and I have time to eat quickly and do the dishes."

As Katie ushered her brothers back into the house, she glanced over her shoulder and said, "Have a good evening. Ramon's meeting is usually over at ten, so we won't be home until after that. We'll check on you when we get back."

"Great," Alana said. "Call if you're going to be late. And drive carefully."

Katie brightened. "Will do."

Jesse stopped in front of the open barn door. "Don't forget to phone if Bailey has her baby. Me and Mark think it's going to be a boy, and we can't wait to see it."

"You know," Mark said, his hands resting on his hips, "I was thinking... Maybe you guys ought to take turns sleeping, just like the army guys do when they're on guard duty."

Clay lifted two fingers and gave him a scout's salute.

Alana just smiled and watched them go. "I love those kids."

"I can see why. They've got good hearts. And they truly seem to care for each other." Clay hadn't shared anything like that with his half brothers. Maybe that's why he'd tried so damned hard to prove himself worthy…of love and respect.

And there was another conclusion he'd just come to.

He blew out a sigh, frustrated at how long it took, how hard he had to work to put his life back in order. But at least it was coming along, slowly but surely.

"Are you ready to eat?" Alana asked. "The pot roast will taste a lot better if it's warm."

"I'm more than ready."

They each took a seat in rickety chairs and sat around the makeshift table. Clay cut a glance at Alana and smiled. He had a feeling they were both in for a nice evening—albeit one unlike any they'd ever had before. And, oddly enough, there was something romantic about it, too.

"My grandfather used this desk," Alana said. "He put it in the back corner of the barn and referred to it as his office until he added a room at the back of the house and made a real one."

Her eyes lit up whenever she talked about her grandfather, and Clay couldn't help wondering if he had grandparents himself. It was hard to say since his memory wasn't firing on all cylinders yet. All he knew was that his mother had died and he'd gone to live with his father, a man he'd resented back then. Surely that had changed in time.

While they ate, he urged himself to envision a familiar face or two but came up short.

"Are you finished?" Alana stood and gathered her disposable dinnerware.

"Yes." He'd been so caught up in his thoughts that he'd neglected to praise the meal. "The meat was delicious. And so were the potatoes and carrots. You're a great cook."

Her smile dimpled her cheeks and put a sparkle in her eyes. "Thanks. I didn't used to like spending time in the kitchen, but after I moved here and had to cook for Grandpa, I found an old recipe box that belonged to my grandmother. I had no idea I'd enjoy whipping up some of the food she used to fix."

Alana carried their discarded plates and put them in an empty trash can that sat near the wall where they'd found the desk.

He watched her walk, the sway of her hips until another memory snuck up on him, and he tumbled back into a world he couldn't quite grasp while living in this one.

Dammit, Clayton. I've got enough of a problem with grain-sniffing rats trying to sneak into the barn without you leaving a leftover ham sandwich to draw them in. Take your food scraps into the house.

Clay caught a shadowy vision of a man who

stood about five foot six or seven, short yet bearing an invincible stature. Dark hair, neatly styled. A well-trimmed mustache.

"Are you okay?" Alana asked, breaking the spell.

He glanced up at her, then got to his feet. "Yeah. I'm all right." Then he nodded to the trash can where she'd deposited their dirty dinnerware. "I'll take that and put it in the sealed receptacle at the side of the house. We don't want to attract flies, ants or rodents. While I'm gone, keep an eye on Bailey."

Without waiting for a response, he snatched up the battered old trash can and carried the whole damned thing out of the barn and disposed of it in the covered container at the side of the house. He stopped by the faucet to wash his hands, then dried them by wiping them against his jeans.

He stayed outdoors for a moment, taking in the sight of a nearly full moon and enjoying the familiar sounds of a ranch at night—the chirp of crickets, the whinny of one of several horses in the corral. How he loved being outside by himself on a night like this... Selena was the only horse in Alana's corral.

Another memory, he supposed. Something that gave him a glimpse of the life he'd led in Texas. It seemed that he was a cowboy lawyer, if that made sense.

He shook it off and returned to the barn, where

he found Alana leaning against the stall railing, watching the mare. She turned toward him as he approached and blessed him with a sweet smile that set off a whoosh in his chest. Damn. Her eyes were an amazing shade of green. And in the soft glow of the light overhead, they seemed to sparkle like a cluster of precious gems, emeralds and diamonds.

He closed the distance between them and softly asked, "How's she doing?"

"About the same."

A piece of straw poked out of the curls that tumbled over her shoulders, and he reached to pluck it out. But instead of dropping it to the ground, he continued to hold it as he brushed his knuckles along her cheek.

Her breath caught, and her gaze locked on his. Something sparked between them, lighting a fuse. A short one, it seemed.

He'd promised himself not to kiss her again until he clearly remembered who he was. But try as he might, he couldn't seem to wrap his mind around what could have provoked him to make a vow he wasn't likely to keep.

As her lips parted, kissing her seemed to be his only option. And when he stepped closer, her chin tilted up. He didn't give a damn who he used to be. Instead, he lowered his mouth to hers.

Chapter Ten

Alana slipped into Clay's embrace as if she'd always belonged in his arms, in his life.

As the kiss deepened, the attraction and desire she'd felt for him since that first night they'd met grew too strong, too intense and alluring to ignore.

Yet there was more in play than just lust. An emotion, warm and vital, rose up in her chest, seeping into every nook and cranny of her heart, reaching into tiny crevices where old hurts, dormant for years, lay hidden.

She'd been holding back her feelings for him until his real identity was revealed, until his memory returned. She'd told herself that by doing so, she was just following doctor's orders. But the longer he stayed on the ranch, the more she'd begun to realize she could fall heart over head for him. She'd seen the way he interacted with Mark and Jesse, and it touched her to the core. Even Rascal, Chewie and Licorice seemed to follow him around. It was so easy to conclude that he was a good, kind and honest man—one worthy of her love and trust.

As their tongues continued to mate, their breaths mingling in a knee-buckling kiss, Clay's fingers slid down the slope of her back, bunching the cotton fabric of her dress. Then they trailed down to her derriere, where he gripped her bottom with both hands and drew her closer still.

His erection, strong and hard, pressed into her, his desire for her clear. It would be so easy to throw caution to the wind, to let passion run its course and continue kissing him as if there were no tomorrow. But the sun would come up, and making love tonight was sure to complicate things.

So she released her hold on him and placed both hands on his broad chest, where his heart beat strong and steady. Slowly and reluctantly, she pushed against him and drew her lips from his.

"We shouldn't do this," she said. "At least, not here. Not now."

"You're right." He reached up and brushed a loose strand of her hair from her brow. "You deserve more than a proverbial roll in the hay."

She smiled.

"And to make matters worse," he said, "I don't have any condoms."

They didn't need them. She was already pregnant. Should she tell him now? She'd been wrestling with her deceit since he'd arrived at her door, but he deserved to hear news like that somewhere other than a dusty, drafty old barn.

Then again, birth control wasn't the only reason to use protection. At that realization, her heart sank.

Was that why Clay had come to Montana looking for her? To tell her that he had a sexually transmitted disease and to suggest she be tested?

Then the voice of reason stepped in. No, that wasn't possible. The physician's assistant had ordered blood work at her very first obstetrical appointment. She'd been tested for all kinds of things, including STDs. And she was clean.

Clay reached out and cupped her jaw, drawing her attention back to the here and now. His thumb skimmed her cheek, caressing it and sending her pulse rate end over end like a gymnast's Olympic routine on the mat.

"Whatever is going on between us, whatever we're feeling is only growing stronger. And when the day comes and the time is right, we should be prepared, even if it's spontaneous. So I'll stop by the drugstore after work tomorrow and pick up a box."

Her lips parted, realizing that whether they were in the barn or at the kitchen table, she ought to say something now. But for some dumb reason, the words failed her.

"What's wrong?" he asked. "You look uneasy."

"It's just that… You don't need to…do that."

"I know. But I should. It's going to happen, whether we plan a romantic evening or not."

She couldn't argue with that. And if he didn't stop strumming her cheek, singeing her skin and creating an empty ache in the most feminine part of her body, making love was going to happen much sooner than later.

As if reading her mind, Clay removed his hand from her face and dropped it to his side. "Maybe we should go back in the house and turn on the television. Or find something to do that will distract us."

That sounded wise. But if they were indoors with a bed just down the hall, she'd be even more tempted to take the lead and be the romantic instigator again.

She sucked in a breath, bit down on her bottom lip, then let out a soft sigh. "You're right, Clay.

But I don't want to leave Bailey. Something could go wrong. She might need us…"

He pressed a kiss on her brow. "Okay. Then we'll stay out here. But we may as well be comfortable."

She looked at him, trying to read his gaze, trying to grasp his meaning and coming up empty-handed. "How do you suggest we do that?"

He tossed her a dazzling grin that turned her inside out, then pointed to the blankets she'd left on the bale of straw.

"We can either lay one on the straw in the corner and sit on it picnic-style, or we can drag a couple of bales toward the door and away from Bailey."

Alana turned and looked toward the stall, where the chestnut mare labored. Would Bailey think she was alone if Alana and Clay hung out twenty or more feet away?

"All right," she said. "Lead the way, cowboy."

The last thing Clay had wanted to do was to stop kissing Alana, but reason won out over desire, a desire that had him on fire. He made his way from the back of the barn to the bale of straw where Alana had stacked the folded blankets and grabbed the worn blue one on top. Then he strode toward the door and found an out-of-the-way spot where they could sit and wait.

He shook out the blanket, then spread it out on the floor strewn with dust and hay. While he took a seat, Alana wandered over to the window that looked out into the yard. He studied her as she peered into the star-studded night sky.

She wore a white sweater and a yellow sundress this evening. He found it interesting that she'd shed her usual jeans and baggy shirts for something more feminine. Did the change have anything to do with him and the growing attraction they both clearly felt?

He'd like to think that it did. Not that it really mattered. He found her appealing no matter what she had on.

She looked especially pretty this evening, her dark brown hair hanging loose, tumbling over her shoulders.

He wanted her with all his being. Right here, right now. Or better yet, he'd take her someplace special. Maybe to Paris, to that little hotel with the softest comforters and a view of the Eiffel Tower.

Wait. He'd been to Paris? Yes, to negotiate an international business deal for someone. But he'd been alone in that room.

At the time, he'd thought that was too bad. But he wasn't alone now.

"Aren't you going to sit down?" he asked.

She turned to him, her back to the window,

and smiled. "Yes, but I wanted to wish upon a star first."

"Oh, yeah?" A grin tugged at one side of his lips. "What'd you wish for?"

"I can't tell you," she said, as she approached him. "If I do, it won't come true."

He had a feeling he knew what she'd been hoping for. If so, they were definitely on the same page. Just thinking about that night they'd spent together in Colorado—even if he couldn't remember all of it—stirred his blood. A battered old barn might be a far cry from the luxurious five-star hotel-room suite, but tell that to the pheromones sparking in the air, the desire rushing through his blood.

The memory of the evening they'd met, now stronger than ever, was stirring something else in him. Something soft and tender that lay deep inside for... Well, even if he didn't have amnesia, he suspected that it had been dormant for longer than he could remember.

He watched as Alana scanned the blanket as if seeking the best place for her to sit. She placed her hand on her stomach and smoothed it over a prominent bulge, then took a seat beside him.

Whoa. It had only been a suspicion before, but he was sure of it now. She asked him a question, but he was so stunned by the size of her belly that he didn't hear a word she said.

A fleeting memory crossed his mind—another pregnant belly and an invitation to touch it.

Put your hand here, Clay. You can feel your baby brother move.

A small lump moved across Mama's stomach, and a sense of wonder warmed a young boy's heart. Clay's heart.

His mother had been so excited about the baby—a little boy. Clay had been, too. But then everything went wrong.

The blood. Streaming down his mother's legs. The look of sheer panic on her face. A call to the neighbor. Connie?

Wait here, Connie told him. *I'm sure everything will be okay once I get her to the hospital.*

But it wasn't okay.

Placenta abruption, Connie had explained later. He hadn't understood at the time, but he'd looked it up. The placenta had separated from the uterine wall, and the baby had died.

The heartbreaking memory darkened. Mom wouldn't get out of bed. She wouldn't eat. Not even when he'd fixed her favorite foods. She'd finally gone to see a shrink, who prescribed some heavy-duty antidepressants. But they didn't seem to help.

And then his dad came by.

I need to talk to your mom alone, his father

had said. So Clay had gone into his bedroom and shut the door. But he'd been unable to shut out the sounds. Broken glass. A slamming door. Mom crying.

Clay sucked in a breath. Dad had broken things off with her. Just walked out on them when they'd needed him most. And his mom had emptied the bottle of pills.

He blinked at the vision and shoved it back where it belonged, back where he'd hidden the memory so he could move on with his life and not be chained down because of it.

Alana drew up her knees and smoothed her dress over them, hiding the bulge in her belly. But Clay couldn't seem to tear his thoughts away from the bump.

"I hope you don't think I'm out of line," he said. "Are you pregnant?"

Her face paled, and her lips parted. The question clearly shocked her. And why wouldn't it? A man with any good upbringing didn't come right out and ask a woman if she was expecting a baby. What if she wasn't? It'd be a shame if he hurt her feelings.

She placed her hand over her stomach, caressing it. "Yes, I am."

Was…was *he* the father?

He waited a beat for her to continue, but she

didn't. If the baby was his, wouldn't she have added that little detail?

Before he could decide on a response or come out and ask, the laboring mare nickered, then let out a squeal.

"I'd better check on Bailey," he said, quickly getting to his feet.

In truth, he wasn't worried about the mare. So far any of her behaviors and the noises she made were all pretty normal. But he needed an excuse to put some distance between him and Alana. At least until he could wrap his mind around the troubling question that had just joined all the others now tumbling around in his foggy brain like bumper cars in an amusement park—especially when he wasn't in any position to deal with the answer.

While Clay sauntered toward the stall, all tall and buff and cowboy, Alana fought the urge to follow him and tell him he was the father. Instead, she continued to sit on the blanket, fingering the frayed edge of the hem. An odd expression had crept over his face like an ominous storm cloud moving across the pale winter sky. Did he realize the baby was his?

He hadn't asked, though. He hadn't even hinted that the possibility had crossed his mind.

She was going to have to tell him. Should she broach the subject now?

Maybe, but she wasn't sure how. One option came to mind. *Remember that night in Colorado...?*

No, that wouldn't work. Clay had amnesia and didn't remember much about that night, if anything at all. A man who didn't recall having sex with a woman would think she was trying to pin something on him. Was that why he hadn't come out and asked?

"Alana," Clay called, drawing her from her reverie. "You'd better come here."

She got to her feet and walked to the back of the barn. "Is everything okay?"

"Things are moving along quickly."

She made her way to the stall where Bailey was lying down. Her tail switched, and little hooves were coming out in a gush of liquid— amniotic fluid—followed by the nose. Bailey pushed and strained.

"Is everything okay?" she asked. "Does she need help?"

"No, she's doing fine."

Moments later, the head came out and, next, the rest of the body. Bailey got to her feet, then turned to sniff at her little one, nudging it, licking it.

"Oh, my gosh," Alana said. "That's amazing. Beautiful."

"Yeah. It's pretty cool."

Alana gaped in wonder at the little brown foal, the newest addition to the Rancho Esperanza. "Is it a boy or a girl?"

"It's a filly."

"Right. I'm pretty new to ranching, but I'll catch on." Alana smiled as she studied the little one. "Bailey's a chestnut, but what color would you call the baby—I mean, her filly?"

"I'm not sure yet. Foals aren't usually born the color or shade they'll be when they get older. Once she sheds her foal coat, we'll have a better idea. In fact, when a foal is registered with the American Quarter Horse Association, we usually leave the color blank and fill it out later, after they get their adult coat."

Clay clearly knew a lot about ranches and horses. He must be familiar with registering them. But what did he mean when he said *we*? Had he been referring to a friend, a brother, an investor?

She supposed it didn't matter.

Bailey nudged the newborn with her nose, and the filly tried to stand up, its spindly legs wobbly from its time spent curled in the womb.

Alana gazed in amazement at the miracle of birth. If this colt proved to be the horse Grandpa thought it would be, it would give her a good chance of turning the ranch around.

That is, if after Olivia's complaint was settled, Alana still had a ranch to save. Her heart sank.

Clay looked at her and dropped his smile. "What's the matter? Foals have long legs. She'll be standing and nursing before you know it."

"It's not that."

"Then, what?"

She stole a glance at the man who'd claimed to be an attorney. "My, uh, inheritance is being challenged. I was served with a certified letter the other day."

"What?" Clay tore his gaze from the mare and her baby in the stall and studied Alana intently. "Who's contesting the will? And why?"

"Olivia McGee. She was married to my grandfather's late brother."

"What's her complaint?"

"Apparently, before Grandpa changed his will last December, she and her husband stood to inherit his estate. But after he found me through that DNA site and we met, he insisted upon seeing his attorney and leaving everything to me. It was all his idea. But she's claiming that I took advantage of him."

"If you don't mind, I'd like to look over that letter."

"Sure. Of course." Alana tucked a strand of

hair behind her ear. "This has really been weighing on me, especially since my grandfather's attorney won't be able to speak on my behalf. Apparently, he has dementia."

"That's too bad." Clay furrowed his brow. "Who's Olivia's attorney?"

"Some guy in Kalispell."

"So Olivia lives around here?"

"Actually, she's a neighbor. Well, at least she used to be. She sold her ranch to Adam Hastings, the pompous jerk from Texas who's been trying to buy up a lot of ranches around here. Until that sale went through, Olivia and I shared a property line."

Clay's eye twitched, and the crease in his brow grew deeper. "Hastings?"

"Yeah." Her gut clenched. "Is something wrong?"

He didn't respond right away. Instead, he combed his fingers through his hair and slowly shook his head. "No. I... I'll need to read over that letter and do a little research. But not until tomorrow morning. When I'm fresh."

"All right." She studied him carefully. He appeared uneasy. Worried. And she found that more than a little disconcerting.

"Why don't you go inside and call Katie," Clay suggested. "The boys wanted to know when the filly was born."

"Oh. Yeah. Good idea."

As much as Alana would prefer to remain in the barn, watching Bailey and her sweet baby, she could use a little diversion. Because when an attorney worried about a lawsuit, the client faced an even bigger challenge than they'd once thought.

That being the case, even if Alana had the courage to tell him that he was the father of her baby, now wasn't the time.

So she left Clay to his worries. Once inside the house, she placed the call to Katie and told the boys about the filly. Through their hoots and excited cheers, she could hear Ramon's voice in the background.

"Is that Alana on the line?" he asked.

"Yep," Mark said.

"Can I speak to her for a minute?"

Mark must have handed over the cell phone, because Ramon said, "I was going to call you, but I thought it might be too late."

Alana glanced at the kitchen clock. She usually turned in before nine thirty, but there was a lot going on tonight. "What's up?"

"I heard a rumor I thought you should be aware of."

Her grip on the phone tightened. "What's that?"

"Leon Cunningham contacted the title company to find out if there are any liens against several ranches in the area."

"You mean, the guy who's running against you for mayor?"

"The guy who *was* running against me. He withdrew from the race yesterday, saying he had bigger fish to fry."

With the election only a couple days away?

"So what does Leon and his visit to the title company have to do with me?" she asked.

"Apparently, a roofing company put a mechanic's lien on your ranch."

"A mechanic's lien? What does that mean?"

"It means your grandfather owed money to a roofing company, and they need to be paid before you can sell the property."

Great. Just when she thought her problems couldn't get any worse, life threw her another curve.

"Do you know how much is owed?"

"No, I'm afraid not. I wish I could be more help."

After thanking him and ending the call, she glanced out the window that looked out into the yard. It was dark outside, yet a light burned in the barn. She was tempted to hurry back to the barn and share her troubles with Clay, but maybe she'd better sit this one out. She'd already unloaded a lot on him this evening. And tomorrow morning, she'd be dumping even more when she told him he was going to be a father.

The name Adam Hastings had struck an off-key chord, although Clay couldn't quite put his finger on why. Somehow, he and Hastings had a connection of some kind. And his gut had twisted into a knot when Alana had referred to the guy as a pompous jerk.

He tried to cobble together what few pieces of his past he'd managed to remember, but he wasn't having much luck. At least Alana had gone into the house, leaving him alone so he could sort through it all.

Over the past few days, he'd begun to remember things, but he hadn't shared any of that with Alana. He wanted to make his way through the briar and the brambles in his brain on his own. And once he'd gotten it all straight, he'd tell her.

Moments ago, he'd been struggling with her pregnancy. But now he didn't find that nearly as concerning as the cryptic revelation that a Texan was buying up multiple ranches in Montana.

And for some damned reason, that was doing a bigger number on his brain than the tire iron.

Damn. A tire iron. He stiffened as the realization slammed his brain so hard he felt as if he'd been struck again. He'd been standing on the side of the road. Car trouble? He'd heard footsteps, and when he'd turned, that someone had clobbered him.

But who?

And why?

He had no idea.

Rather than remain in the barn, where Alana, Katie and the boys would soon be joining him, he decided to turn in for the night. Mare and foal appeared to be doing just fine, so he left them alone and headed for the back door.

He found Alana in the kitchen, where she'd ended the phone call. She turned to him, her brow creased.

"I'm beat," he said. "Sam's been insisting that he needs to take inventory, and his wife asked if I would mind doing it for him. Since I'm going to get started at five, I'm going to bed." Without waiting for her to answer, he hurried to his room.

Only trouble was, he didn't sleep worth a damn. He spent the night going over various portions of his memories like a man hard at work trying to put the pieces of a giant jigsaw puzzle in place.

And he didn't like the picture that began to take shape.

By the end of the night, Clay had recalled that he himself had been the result of an affair. When his mother learned that his father was married and cheating on his wife…

His father.

"Oh, no." He squeezed his eyes tight and cursed as the realization smacked him in the face. *Adam Hastings was his father.* The *pompous jerk* buying up Montana ranches.

Clay also remembered that Adam had never left his wife. He *had* stepped up to provide financial support and came to visit at times. But that had been it.

The two of them were never very close, even though Clay had wished they were and craved a warm relationship with a father that never seemed to have time for him.

But that wasn't the end of it. When Clay was twelve, his father's wife had died, and his dad had started coming around to see his mom again. That's when his mom got pregnant.

There was no second chance at a happily-ever-after, though. She'd lost the baby. And then they'd split up. Again. God, how that had crushed her, and she'd fallen apart.

With his memory returning, the pain of losing her was even more acute. A punch to the gut. A knife in his chest.

After she'd died, Clay had moved in with his father and his older half brothers, who weren't happy about having a newfound sibling. One that had come as a complete surprise.

That's about all he remembered. But it was

enough to know that something about his sudden appearance at Rancho Esperanza hadn't been purely to rekindle one night of passion. And he had a hunch that when he finally had all the pieces in order and Alana found out the connection Clay had to his father—and vice versa—all hell was going to break loose.

Adam Hastings sat at the polished cherrywood desk in his private office on the Double H Ranch having his second cup of coffee while going over a portfolio from one of his investment bankers. He reached over to the calculator and ran a few numbers himself. He'd just hit Total when his phone buzzed, alerting him that Rosina, his private secretary, needed him for one thing or another.

It'd better be more important than the last time she'd interrupted him. "Yes. What is it?"

"Sir, a car-rental company in Montana is on the other line. It seems that your son leased a vehicle several weeks ago. He told them he only needed it for a few days, but he hasn't returned it yet or called to extend the agreement."

What the hell? Adam ran a hand through his thinning hair. Clayton had flown to Montana and asked Adam to trust him, to let him work things out on his own. And so he'd given his youngest son free rein.

It wasn't like him to be irresponsible. He reached for his cell and called, only to learn Clay's voice mail was full. Again, that wasn't at all like him.

He pushed the intercom button and buzzed Rosina. When she answered he asked, "Have you talked to Clayton recently?"

"Not for a few weeks. Not since he told me he was taking a vacation to do some fishing."

Clayton was a stickler for details—and honest to a fault. He wouldn't have kept the car longer than he'd agreed to without contacting the rental company. Not unless something had gone wrong.

An uneasy feeling settled over him. As a kid, Clayton had been an inconvenience. But as an adult, he'd proven himself to be trustworthy and dependable. Unlike the other two boys—God love 'em—Clay had become an asset to the family rather than an embarrassment. And the thought that something might have happened to him…

Or had Clay gotten distracted by his latest assignment?

Adam grinned at the thought. He remembered the conversation they'd had four months ago, when he'd first sent Clayton to that cattle symposium in Colorado.

This land deal is very important to me. And to

this family. Just make it happen. I don't care how you do it. Hell, charm the pants off her.

At that, Clayton had gotten self-righteous and bent out of shape. *I'll close the deal, but I won't resort to seduction.*

Dammit, Clayton. Don't get your hackles up. It's just a figure of speech. The last thing I want you to do is hop into bed with that woman.

But hell, if that's what it took, so be it. Maybe Clayton had more of the Hastings's gumption running in his veins than he liked to believe.

"Mr. Hastings," Rosina said, "do you want me to call the private investigator you've used in the past?"

"No, don't bother. I'll do the investigating myself. Just get me a first-class ticket to Kalispell, Montana."

Chapter Eleven

By the time Alana woke up, Clay had already eaten breakfast, fed the animals and gone to work. She'd hoped to talk to him before he left. Something had been off last night, after he'd come in from the barn and before he'd gone to bed. Then again, she'd been so troubled by news of the lien on the ranch that she might have been mistaken about that.

She filled the teapot with water. One thing she did know was that she was going to tell him about the baby when he got home.

Just after eight o'clock, Katie and the boys joined Alana in the kitchen but only long enough to fix themselves three bowls of cereal. They had plans to attend an all-day scouting event in Ka-lispell and were eager to join their friends. The troop leader had even roped Katie into staffing one of the booths.

"Are you sure you don't want to go with us?" Katie asked Alana, as she and the boys prepared to leave.

"It sounds like it'll be a fun day," Alana said, "but I've got a lot to do. I have to go to the mar-ket, the laundry is piling up and I have some bills to pay."

"That sounds boring," Jesse said.

"Maybe. But it'll feel good when I'm fin-ished." Actually, she was looking forward to having some time to herself. There were a few things she wanted to scratch off her to-do list—like organizing Grandpa's weird filing system in the office. And, while she was at it, she would be looking for any paperwork pertaining to roof repair.

So that's the first thing she focused on—finding something to help explain who'd filed a lien on the ranch and why it hadn't been released.

She'd worked through the lunch hour and finally found a bill from Flannigan's Roofing Company. It had been marked Paid and filed away. And when she went through the old bank statements, she found that the check had cleared the bank.

A phone call to the roofer didn't provide any help, either. The bookkeeper was out of the office until next week, and no one else seemed to know anything.

At least the back property taxes Grandpa had owed were no longer hanging over her head, but that lien and any interest or fines could be a major problem. And then there was the news that Olivia was contesting the will. Talk about being backed into a corner. But she'd find a way out.

She needed to talk to someone—and before her appointment with the woman lawyer on Monday. Too bad Henry Dahlberg wouldn't be any help. Did she dare dump it on Clay when he got home tonight?

He might not mind. And he could have some solid advice. He seemed to like living here. He'd also been helping out a lot. Maybe he'd feel bad if she didn't ask his opinion. Besides, he claimed to be an attorney, even if he seemed more like a rancher. And a wealthy one at that.

For the rest of the day, Alana kept herself busy, doing one chore or another. But she couldn't help wandering out to the barn to check on Bailey and Buttercup, the name she'd chosen for the foal. At one time, she'd thought she might sell the filly, but in less than twenty-four hours, she'd become too attached to the sweet little thing to let it go.

Speaking of sweet little things, she'd definitely

have to tell Clay tonight. She placed her hand over her baby bump, which had grown considerably over the past couple of weeks since Clay's arrival. Only trouble was, which news should she give him first?

As she puttered around the kitchen, pulling out the ingredients she'd need to make spaghetti, Rascal and Licorice began to bark. She glanced out the window and spotted an unfamiliar white car pulling into the yard. A man dressed in shiny black boots and a Western-style suit got out of the driver's seat. He reached back inside, pulled out a fancy cowboy hat and placed it on his head.

"That's odd," she muttered, as she walked outside to see who the guy was and what he wanted.

"Can I help you?" she asked.

The rather handsome gentleman, who appeared to be in his sixties, flashed her a charming smile. "I hope so." He approached with an outstretched hand. "You must be Ms. Perez. We've never met in person, but I'm Adam Hastings."

Alana nearly rolled her eyes at the guy. As if her life couldn't get any worse. But then again, she'd come to expect it to throw a curve ball her way.

"I'm afraid you've made a trip for nothing, Mr. Hastings. I'm not interested in selling my ranch." Heck, she wasn't even sure how long she'd even have a ranch.

"So you've told me on several occasions." Again, he smiled as if that's all it would take to make her see reason. "I find that surprising since I've offered you considerably more than it's worth."

She folded her arms across her chest. "You see a run-down ranch, a house that needs repair and an almost nonexistent cattle herd, but I see a gold mine." What she didn't say was that it was going to kill her to give it up and hand it over to Olivia.

"Actually," he said, "I didn't come here to up my offer. I came looking for my son. I thought you might tell me where I can find him."

His son? How the heck would she know? "I'm sorry, but I have no idea what you're talking about."

"You *should*," he said. "Clayton Hastings. You met in Colorado. At the cattle symposium."

Alana's heart dropped to the pit of her stomach and ground against the inner lining like a ceramic pestle crushing a pill in a mortar, a pill that was too bitter to swallow.

There had to be a mistake. Clay wasn't, couldn't be... But then she saw it. The older man had the same color eyes, the same cut of the chin.

As the familiar sound of a battered pickup engine grew louder, she tore her gaze from the wealthy Texas jerk who'd been determined to buy her ranch and looked down the graveled drive.

She stood statue still, her arms at her sides, her hands clenched, fingernails sharp against her palms. If her Clay turned out to be Adam Hastings's son, and it certainly appeared that way, then he'd been up to no-good when they'd met in Colorado. She couldn't believe theirs had been a chance encounter. A fluke.

Time would tell, she supposed. And the clock had run out on the lies.

All of them.

Clay couldn't wait to get back to the ranch. He hadn't slept worth a damn last night, and he'd been at work since dawn, so he was exhausted. He wasn't especially hungry, though. Sam's wife had stopped by and brought him lunch—homemade tacos, refried beans and rice—which had filled him up. So after a hot, invigorating shower, he might pass on dinner altogether.

But he needed to talk to Alana, to tell her that he'd begun remembering things, even if they were still pretty confusing. Maybe it would be an easier conversation for them to have if they were sitting at the kitchen table.

As he pulled into the yard, he spotted a late-model white Mercedes and a man facing the front porch, where Alana stood, her eyes on him, her expression somber.

Something was clearly wrong, although he'd

be damned if he could figure it out from here. He'd no more than climbed out of the pickup when Rascal and Licorice came running up to greet him, tails wagging. He gave them each a half-hearted scratch on the head.

The man turned and broke into a grin. "There you are, Clayton. I've been worried about you."

Who...? The question had barely registered when familiarity snuck up on him. Those eyes that lit up with pride. The pride young Clayton had always sought. Still, he voiced a tentative question. "Dad?"

"Something wrong with your eyes?"

Recognition slammed into Clay, stealing the air from his lungs as memories bombarded him like pelting rocks.

Riding fence on the Double H with the hands. Raul. Sonny. Jimbo... Roping contests. Horse races. Titan, the gelding he kept in the Double H stables, was fast.

His father strode toward him and scrunched his brow as he gave him a once-over. "Whoa. You really got into the part, didn't you, son? Where'd you get those clothes? The Goodwill? That old pickup is a nice touch, too."

Clay frowned. A part? His father thought he was playing a part? Damn. He'd wanted to believe that he'd come to Rancho Esperanza looking for Alana for his own reasons, personal ones.

But it was sounding as if… As if he'd been sent on a mission.

His gut clenched at the thought, twisting upward until it squeezed the air from his lungs and the words from his mouth.

Dad's lips quirked into a crooked smile, and he slowly shook his head. "You look like a ranch hand."

He'd said it as if it was a bad thing. But it didn't feel like that. Should it?

His father chuffed. "Hell, I don't know *what* you've been up to, Clayton, but you failed to check in, so I had come on up here to Montana. But what do you know? Before I even found you, I ran into Alana here, and she's informed me that she still doesn't want to sell."

No, she didn't. She wouldn't.

"And I was just about to tell her that she'd be able to purchase a nice home in town—free and clear," his old man added. "No mortgage hanging over her head. No repairs to make."

Clay cut a glance at Alana, her green eyes ablaze, her lips drawn tight.

I can explain, he wanted to say. But how could he do that when he still wasn't entirely sure what he was doing here or why he'd come in the first place? Oddly enough, as the seconds ticked on, and the puzzle pieces began to fall into place, it all began to make sense.

This land deal is very important to me. And to this family. Just make it happen. I don't care how you do it. Hell, charm the pants off of her."

Bile in Clay's belly churned. Is that what he'd done in Colorado? Had he seduced Alana in order to get her to sell the ranch?

No, that didn't feel right. But he couldn't very well stand here gaping at Alana and his father, unable to explain or defend himself—assuming there was a defense to be had.

"Dad," Clay said, "let's go for a drive. You and I need to talk."

Then he looked at Alana, who seemed utterly aghast.

"I'll be back," he told her. "And I'll explain everything." But could he? The claim seemed feeble at best.

She didn't say a word. She just watched him circle the car and climb into the passenger seat. Then she walked back into the house and slammed the door.

And right now, he couldn't blame her.

Alana stood just inside the house, her back to the door. A sense of betrayal swept over her, making her sick, and she bit back the nausea.

How could she have been so stupid, so gullible? She swore under her breath. And she *never* swore. But if a day ever deserved a string of four-letter words, it was today.

Clay didn't seem to have any memory issues now. At least, he hadn't had any problem recognizing Adam Hastings, who just happened to be his *father*.

Tears stung her eyes, and she blinked them back to no avail. She'd once thought their meeting in Colorado had been serendipitous, but she'd been wrong. He'd been looking for her to do his father's bidding. And he'd found her.

She had half a notion to march down the hall, pack his bags and place them in the yard. Only thing was, he didn't have any things. No wallet, no suitcase, no clothes that would do him any good on a ranch. She'd given him Grandpa's shirts and jeans. She'd even bought him a toothbrush.

Damn him. She marched to the mudroom, where she found an empty cardboard box, then she carried it to his quarters. She threw everything into it: his stupid toothbrush, the nearly new bar of soap he'd been using, Grandpa's razor, shaving cream—all of it. Even the borrowed clothing. And when she had everything packed away—and not the least bit neatly—she toted the carton out the front door and left it in the yard.

He'd get the picture. He wasn't welcome here. Not anymore. And not ever again.

Then she strode back to the house and locked the door. It felt good to be rid of him. Real good. But as the anger began to subside, a searing grief took its place. He'd broken her heart, but what did she expect? A fairy-tale ending?

She was too trusting. And stupid. She should have known better. All Clay had wanted was to buy her ranch. And neither she nor Rancho Esperanza were for sale.

Only trouble was, would Clay want to claim her baby as his? And if so, how would that play into the scheme of things?

"Where are we going, Clayton?"

"Just drive."

His father gunned the engine, hightailing it away from Rancho Esperanza. "Suppose you tell me what's going on."

"That's not going to be easy to explain, so you'll have to bear with me. To be completely honest, I'm not entirely sure why I'm in Montana. But shortly after I arrived in Fairborn, I was carjacked. Someone damn near killed me, but as you can see, I survived." He fingered the scar on his head. "Unfortunately, I've had amnesia for the past couple of weeks, although things are just now beginning to come together."

"Seriously?" His father shot a glance at him. "Are you okay?"

"Yeah. At least, physically. I've still got some confusion to sort through.

"Am I supposed to believe that you've been living with that woman and that you forgot why you were here?" His father clucked his tongue. "I hope that doesn't mean you dropped the ball."

Clay slowly shook his head in disbelief. "Dad, I couldn't even recall what ball I was supposed to be holding." Until today, he hadn't remembered enough yet to know whether he'd screwed up or not. "I've been staying on the ranch with her, but I'm not sleeping with her, if that's what you mean."

His father snorted, clearly skeptical. And Clay couldn't really blame him. If Clay were to stay much longer, the sleeping arrangements could easily change.

"I've gained her trust," Clay added. "Or at least I had, before you showed up." But whose trust did he really want to gain? He wasn't entirely sure.

"Like I said, son, I was worried."

About Clay? Or about the deal he'd been sent to close? Before either of them spoke, a snippet of a past conversation came to mind.

That particular ranch is the key to my new real estate venture. The state is very likely to build a new highway through that area. And if that happens, a couple more towns are bound to pop up and the land values are going to quadruple—at the very least.

Damn. Was his father trying to cash in on the deal before the news leaked? If so, it sounded like political corruption. Surely Clay hadn't gone along with his father's scheme.

"If you were Artie or Phil," Dad said, "I wouldn't have been as worried. Shoot, they ended up being disappointments in the long run. But you turned out to be a nice surprise. You're a lot more like me than they are."

Several weeks ago, before the tire iron knocked him senseless, that was just the type of acceptance and praise he'd wanted to hear. Now *that*, he could remember.

But now? The fact that he might have more of his father's DNA than his half brothers churned in his gut.

"I thought you would have convinced her to sell by now. What's the holdup?"

"Are you really that thickheaded?" Clay sent his father a disbelieving glance. "I already told you I've had amnesia. And that someone tried to kill me. Isn't that reason enough for a delay?"

His father let out a grunt. "Sure. Of course it is. I'm glad you're okay, son."

"On top of that, Dad, I've come to respect Alana. She's not only attractive, she also has a good heart. I really like her." That was true, although his feelings for her ran a lot deeper than that. And if she was carrying his baby, like he'd come to suspect, she'd be a part of his life for a long time, which pleased him

"At any rate," Clay said, "she's not going anywhere. No matter how much you offer her. That ranch isn't for sale. And your plan to buy it is dead in the water."

His old man slowly shook his head, his disgust evident in the look on his face. "I take it back. You're not as strong as I am."

"That's not a bad thing."

"I think it is." His father gripped the wheel and stared out the windshield, his plan to gain the title to Rancho Esperanza apparently as strong as ever. "Especially when you don't have a backbone."

Somehow, that didn't ring true.

"You know what I *do* remember?" Clay asked the man. "Doing my best to make you proud, to prove myself worthy of you and my new family. I learned everything I could about cattle and ranching. And I busted my butt on the ball field and in the classroom. I always knew I'd never earn your love, but I settled for your respect and acceptance."

"You've always had it."

He'd never felt it.

His father let out a sigh. "Your early years were complicated, Clayton."

Marital infidelity certainly was. So was introducing an illegitimate son to his older brothers, teenagers who'd never known he existed until his father brought him home one day and told them their new brother was here to stay.

"Did you ever stop to realize that I loved ranching?" Clay asked. "I would have given anything to work on the Double H, but you insisted I get a law degree. So I did it, even though I never really had any interest in being an attorney."

"You may not have the interest, but you're a damned good one."

Clay supposed that was true. But he would have made a good rancher, too. And he would have been a lot happier. He was tempted to tell his father that he was done trying to gain his love and respect, that he wasn't going to be the family attorney any longer, but this wasn't the right time. His brains were still a little scrambled, his thoughts still too disjointed. When he broached a subject like that, he needed to be clear minded.

He also needed to talk to Alana, to explain himself—and to tell her he'd come to care for her. Deeply. And he'd come to think that way about the baby, too, even if it wasn't his. The baby wouldn't have to know that. As far as he was concerned, it was *theirs*.

"Listen," Clay said. "Go back to Texas. Let me work things out here."

"But you just told me she's never going to sell."

Clay looked out the window, at the passing scenery, the green fields, the stacks of hay. "I've got a plan. Okay? I just need more time." More time to think. More time to actually come up with a strategy.

As they continued on a drive to nowhere in particular, Clay cut a glance across the seat. "How'd you get here, Dad?"

"Ryan borrowed the company plane and took some of his friends to attend a bachelor party in Vegas. So I flew commercially. Why?"

"Because I'm going to drop you off at the airport. If you can't get a flight back to Texas tonight, you can charter a plane. I'm going to need to keep this car for a few more days."

"Oh, yeah? You got it all worked out, huh?"

Not really. But he was working on it.

"Okay," his father said. "But speaking of cars, the rental company you used in Kalispell called the office and told Rosina that you hadn't returned their Range Rover. And you didn't contact them to extend the contract. Where's that vehicle?"

Clay sucked in a breath and blew it out. "The amnesia. Remember? I was carjacked. Have Rosina give the company a call and report it stolen. And since I wouldn't have left home without my personal credit card, it's safe to assume that ended up in the wrong hands, too."

"We'd better file a police report, too."

"I've already got that on my to-do list. Will you ask Rosina to contact Visa for me? In the meantime, I'm out of cash and could use a loan."

His father chuffed, a frustrated sound, but at the same time, a crooked grin crinkled his eyes. "Damn, Clayton. You're beginning to sound like your older brothers did back in their college days."

Yeah, well, Clay felt like a college kid right now—living and learning. Yet when it was all said and done, he hoped he'd have a second degree, this one in dealing with life's bigger problems.

Without batting an eye, Dad reached inside his custom, tailor-made jacket, felt around for the pocket and pulled out a wad of bills held in a solid-gold money clip. "Will a thousand bucks do?"

For starters. "Thanks."

After peeling off ten one hundred dollar bills, his father whipped out a platinum Visa. "Take the company card. Don't lose this one."

"I won't." Clay slipped it into his pocket. Then, using his father's smartphone, he found a late-night flight to Houston. "There aren't any first-class seats available."

His father swore under his breath. "I hate flying coach. I just might charter a flight."

Forty-five minutes later, they pulled into the airport and stopped at the curb. While the car was parked and the engine was idling, his father got out from behind the wheel, opened the trunk and pulled out a small Louis Vuitton bag. Clay circled the vehicle, climbed into the driver's seat and rolled down the window. "Have a nice flight, Dad."

"Keep me posted."

"I will."

His father turned to go, then stopped. "When do you expect to be home?"

Clay remembered now. He had a home. A condominium in downtown Houston with white walls, leather couches and chairs. A few pieces of brightly colored Southwestern art. Not much more. But it no longer felt like a place to permanently hang his hat.

"I'm not sure," he said. "It depends."

His thoughts drifted to Alana, to the angry expression she'd worn when he'd left her without an explanation. And he couldn't blame her. The revelations had to have rocked her world entirely— especially that he was Adam Hastings's son. And she'd probably assumed that he'd come to see her under false pretenses.

She didn't seem like the type to hold a grudge. Hopefully, she wouldn't feel like holding one now.

But nearly an hour later, when Clay arrived at Rancho Esperanza, the headlights illuminated the yard where a cardboard box sat, halfway between the house and the barn. The sleeve of the blue plaid Western shirt he'd worn yesterday was draped over the side.

He got out of the car, expecting the dogs to greet him, but apparently they were with the boys—or in the ranch house with Alana. He strode over to the box and peered inside. A bar of soap. The shampoo from his shower. His toothbrush.

Damn. Alana had certainly let him know where he stood. Up to his knees in it.

He headed for the porch, climbed the steps and tried to open the front door, only to find it locked. So he knocked, loud and firm.

From inside, the dogs barked, alerting Alana to his arrival. He waited for her to answer, but as the seconds ticked out, he realized she wasn't in any hurry to let him in.

Still, he stood patiently, doing his best to tamp down a growing sense of guilt and remorse.

Finally, the porch light came on. Then the

door cracked open. Her body, draped in a pale blue robe, blocked his entrance. One look at her puffy tear-stained face, her red-rimmed eyes and turned-down lips and his efforts to ease his remorse failed miserably.

"I'm sorry," he said. "I know I hurt you, but it was unintentional. Can I come in and explain?"

Her hand gripped the side of the door, the knuckles white. "No, Clay. There's nothing more for you to say. I've heard enough already."

He raked a hand through his hair, as if that might clear his somewhat muddled brain and help him dredge up the right words. "I should have told you that my memory was coming back to me, but it came in pieces I had to sort through. Trust me, I never expected my father to show up here. But I didn't know he was my father—or what my name was—until today. And actually, I'm still trying to make sense of things."

"I don't have anything to sort out," she said. "You and your father are in cahoots."

"Not really. I mean, our relationship isn't like that. At least, I don't think it is."

She nodded toward the driveway. "I see you have a vehicle at your disposal. So please get off my property and go back to wherever you came from."

"All right," he said. "But I'm not going very far. I'll be back. We need to talk."

"Yes, we do. But not tonight."

He took that as a sign that she'd eventually listen to what he had to say. "Tomorrow, then."

She let out a heavy sigh. "Clay, as much as I'd like to shut you out of my life forever, I don't think I can."

That was another good sign. Right?

"I'm having your baby, Clay."

He'd known that. Or at least, strongly suspected it. But the revelation now nearly floored him. Unnerved him. Scared him, too. He couldn't help thinking about his mother and the baby she'd lost.

"Have you seen a doctor?" he asked. "I mean, is everything okay?"

"Yes, I have. And everything is as it should be."

With her pregnancy, maybe. But things weren't okay as far as the two of them.

He nodded and took a step back. He'd give her some space and time. Hell, he needed some time, too.

"As much as I would have liked to have kept my child's paternity a secret, you deserve to know. But don't worry. I don't need you or your money. And I sure as hell don't need your father's, either." Then she shut the door soundly and clicked the deadbolt into place.

Chapter Twelve

Damn. Could Clay's puzzling life get any more complicated? Not that he doubted Alana. It's just that this news, and oddly heartwarming as it was, meant that…

Oh, hell. He had no idea what it meant.

Up ahead, a red vacancy light flickered under a sign that read Marty's Motor Inn. A café called The Wagon Wheel sat across the parking lot, where several big rigs were parked.

He needed a place to spend the night, and this would have to do. At least it wasn't too far from the ranch. So he turned into the driveway and parked next to a light blue minivan and a red Toyota pickup.

Then, after retrieving his box from the back seat, he carried it into the office, where he handed the ruddy-faced clerk the company credit card.

"Here you go," the clerk said, as he gave Clay the key—the old style you actually had to stick into the lock on the door—to room ten. "It's the one closest to the café. If you're hungry, the food's pretty good."

Clay thanked him, then left the office. The Mexican feast he'd had at lunch, followed by his dad's untimely arrival, Alana's anger and her announcement that he actually was going to be a father, had wiped out any hunger pangs he might have had. So he went directly to his room.

Marty's Motor Inn didn't provide the kind of lodging he was used to when traveling for pleasure or business, but the room was clean and the bed was comfortable.

Hopefully, by the time morning rolled around, he'd be able to come up with the game plan he'd told his father he had.

Charm her. Do whatever it takes. Just convince her that it's in her best interest to take the money I'm offering her and buy a nice place in town, something she won't have to repair or renovate. I'll be doing her a favor.

Is that why he'd been in Colorado? Had he gone looking for Alana to do his father's bidding?

The possibility turned his stomach. That is, until his memory kicked into gear again.

Long wavy black hair tumbled over her shoulders. Big green eyes framed in thick dark lashes. A light scatter of freckles across her nose. A bow-shaped mouth, pink and glossy after a fresh application of lipstick...

Talk about instant attraction.

He bought her a drink and one led to another. He didn't plan to get her drunk. He just enjoyed listening to the sound of her voice, the lilt of her laugh. The longer he sat across from her, the more she impressed him in all the right ways. And as the evening wore on...he found his loyalty, which had always been to his father, shifting.

As his memory of that night grew stronger, the clearer things became. Sure, he'd met up with Alana, just as his father had asked. But while he'd gladly taken her to his hotel room, making love with her had nothing to do with swaying her. It had been a mutual decision that hadn't had anything to do with her selling the ranch.

Clay took a seat on the edge of the bed and scrubbed a hand over his face as he again pondered the evening in question, beginning with the first time he saw her seated at that cocktail table by herself and the slow realization he'd come to after hearing how important the ranch was to her.

And that shift in his loyalty that began that

night was now complete. The more time he'd spent with her on the ranch, the more he'd gotten to know her, he'd come to realize just how much the property meant to her, no matter the shape it was in or the value placed upon it.

He would encourage her not to sell it to his father at any price, but she still stood to lose it, which would crush her. It would crush him, too, because he didn't want to see her suffer what was sure to be a brutal emotional blow. So he would stand by her through it all and help in any way he could.

Bottom line? Despite his motives for coming to the ranch in the first place, he loved her. He respected her. He didn't need to be hit in the head to know that. And now that she was having his baby, he was more determined than ever to stand by her side.

Oddly enough, coming up with a game plan hadn't taken him nearly as long as he'd thought it would. From now on, he no longer had anything to prove to his father. Instead, he'd have to prove himself to Alana.

How hard could that be?

He had a strong moral code, even though his father seemed to challenge it at every turn, and from this night forward, he would be more vocal when it came to calling his father's business dealings as he saw them.

If the old man didn't like it, he'd have to find another personal attorney. And if that meant he cut Clay out of the will, so be it. Some things were more important than money. Alana had taught him that.

He turned down the sheets and stretched out on the bed, a strategy finally coming together. When the sun came up, he was going to make things right.

After a morning shower, Clay checked out of Marty's Motor Inn and headed into town. He grabbed a quick bite to eat at the café next door, then drove to Callie and Ramon's house, which was located on a quiet street several blocks off Main.

Clay rang the bell, and Ramon answered. He frowned when he saw who stood on the stoop. "What do you want?"

"I see that Alana has already talked to you," Clay said.

"She talked to Callie for more than an hour last night. So, yeah. We know who you really are. And why you came to Fairborn."

"Listen," Clay said, "I don't blame you for being skeptical, but if you give me some time, I'll prove myself worthy of Alana."

"I hope you do." Ramon folded his arms across

his chest, clearly not about to invite him inside. "But what can I do for you now?"

"Do you know where Henry Dahlberg lives? I need to talk to him."

"That's probably going to be a waste of time," Ramon said.

"So I've heard. But I'd still like to ask him a couple of questions."

Ramon gave him the address, and ten minutes later, Clay was standing on the porch of a beige two-story house with white trim and a red door. He knocked, and a woman in her early seventies and using a cane answered.

"Can I help you?" she asked.

"I hope so. I'm looking for Mr. Dahlberg."

"I'm afraid he's napping. He's recovering from surgery and needs his rest. I'm Doris Dahlberg, his wife."

Clay introduced himself. "I'm an attorney, but I'm also a friend of Alana Perez. Your husband prepared her grandfather's will."

"That's right. Henry and Jack McGee were old friends. In fact, my husband prepared all three of Jack's wills."

"*Three*?"

"That's right."

"Are you sure?"

She smiled proudly and nodded, the silvery strands in her hair glistening in the morning sunlight. "I worked with my husband ever since we got married, back in 1981. So I'm familiar with most of his clients and the work he did for them. I was out on disability leave when Alana came to the office, but my husband kept me in the loop."

Talk about a stroke of luck. Alana had a witness who could corroborate her story.

"Please, come in," Doris said, as she turned and limped to a floral-printed, overstuffed chair. "Have a seat and make yourself comfortable."

Clay closed the door and sat on the matching sofa that faced her chair. "So you and your husband are both retired?"

"I suppose you could say that, although we'd planned to work another year or two. I had a knee replacement last winter, then got an infection and had to have it redone. So I took some time off to heal, and Henry hired a woman from the temp agency to fill in for me. But I was working the day Henry came in and told Jack that he'd met his granddaughter, and he was ecstatic. You see, he and his late wife only had one child—a daughter they both adored. But they had a falling out years ago." She leaned back in the chair. "Well, if you're Alana's friend, you probably know all about that."

"Yes, some of it. She and her grandfather found each other through a DNA registry site."

"That was a real blessing. Jack hadn't been

very happy the last few years. And he'd been lonely after his wife died." She sobered. "But I get the feeling that's not why you're here."

"You're right," Clay said. "I had a few questions I wanted to ask your husband, but I heard he was having a few memory issues."

"That's true. We thought he was coming down with Alzheimer's or the like. Turns out it was a brain tumor. Benign—thank the Lord—and they got it all."

"I'm glad to hear that," Clay said.

"Since I was his paralegal, I might be able to answer your questions."

"I hope you can," Clay said. "Olivia McGee claims that Alana took advantage of Jack when he was sick and on pain medication. She's contesting the will."

"That's a shame," Doris said. "I have to admit, Henry's memory isn't quite up to snuff, so he might not be a good witness for Alana. But I'd be happy to set the record straight as much as I can."

"That's good to know," Clay said. "What can you tell me?"

Doris placed her hands on the edge of both armrests and sat forward. "Jack originally left his estate to his brother, Larry. But six years ago, after Larry died, Jack changed the will."

"Oh, yeah? Why's that?"

"Jack loved his brother. But he never did like

Olivia. Thought she was a gold digger. So he told Henry he'd be damned if he'd leave that woman anything. So he decided to give everything to the Boys & Girls Club in Kalispell. But then he told us how he'd found Alana through that DNA website. We'd never seen him so happy. That is, not in the years after Janice, his daughter and only child, ran off. He loved that girl with all his heart, and when she up and eloped with the Perez boy, it darn near killed him."

"So that's why he changed his will a third time and left everything to Alana?"

"You got that right. She's a good girl. A lot like her mama used to be. But not likely to chase after a loser."

No, Clay thought. That wasn't at all likely. And all he had to do was convince Alana that he wasn't the kind of man she thought he was.

"If I go back to the office," Doris said, "I can give you a copy of the three wills. Henry was of sound mind for all of them, even the one he did just after Jack found Alana—I can vouch for that."

"That would be great."

"Better yet…" Doris broke into a grin. "I've been converting Henry's documents into electronic files, and I can email those wills to you."

"I'd appreciate it. And so will Alana. Thank you."

"Can I offer you a cup of coffee?" she asked.

"Or maybe a glass of sweet tea? It won't take me long."

"I don't mind waiting. And sweet tea sounds good."

Thirty minutes later, Clay drove to Kalispell to see Darrell Grimes, Olivia's attorney. Fortunately, the heavy-set older man had time to see Clay and invited him back to his private office.

Once Clay was seated in front of the man's polished oak desk, he said, "I'm not sure if you know this, but your client is going to battle without any bullets."

"What makes you say that?"

Clay told him what he'd learned from Doris Dahlberg. "I can provide you with copies of all three wills."

"You don't say." Darrell leaned back in his leather chair, the springs creaking from the strain of his girth, and folded his arms across his chest. "I truly believed Mrs. McGee's claim, that your friend Alana had taken advantage of a lonely old man. And that she'd used an old small-town lawyer who was suffering from dementia to help her pull it off. But apparently, my client doesn't have a leg to stand on. I'll give her a call and suggest that she drop the case."

Clay hoped Olivia would take her attorney's advice. Either way, Alana had a strong case. And he couldn't wait to tell her.

* * *

Alana woke early on Tuesday, eager to drive into town and to cast her vote for Ramon. Leon may have dropped out of the race, which meant Ramon was sure to win, but she wanted to show her complete support of Callie's new husband. Then she drove home and spent the rest of the morning cleaning out the bedroom where Clay had once slept, determined to turn it into a nursery. That is, if she was still living at Rancho Esperanza when the baby was born.

She'd no more than packed up the last of Grandpa's clothing into a box when Rascal and Licorice began to bark, letting her know someone had driven into the yard.

She didn't have to look out the window to know it was Clay. She'd figured he'd come back, especially since she'd told him she was pregnant with his baby. And while she wasn't ready to talk to him, like it or not, she'd probably be tied to him in one way or another for the next eighteen years, so she'd better get used to dealing with him.

After taking a deep, fortifying breath, she went to the front door, where she found him standing on the porch, his hat in hand. One that hadn't belonged to Grandpa. His shirt and jeans were new, too.

"What do you want?" she asked—and not very nicely.

"We need to talk about a lot of things, mostly the baby. But first, I'd like to solve your dilemma."

He was her biggest dilemma. She crossed her arms, resting them on her baby bump. "I'm not selling my ranch."

"I know that. I'm not offering to buy it."

"Okay. I'm listening."

He handed her a letter, similar to the one the process server had given her from Olivia's attorney.

She cocked her head slightly and frowned. "What's this?"

"A letter stating that Olivia McGee is dropping the case."

As much as she'd wanted to punch Clay's lights out last night and wail at him earlier this morning, she couldn't help but soften. "Are you sure?"

"I spoke to her attorney this morning. I also talked to Doris Dahlberg, Henry's wife and paralegal. Olivia's claims are completely unmerited, and Doris would have been happy to testify in your defense if Olivia hadn't agreed to withdraw her suit."

"I…" Alana glanced down at the letter in her

hands, at the law firm's return address. "I don't know what to say."

"Rest assured, Alana, no one is going to take this ranch away from you."

"But what about the lien?" she asked, hesitant to believe him yet desperate to hang on to the best news she'd heard in months.

"I stopped by the roofing company, too. It appears that one of their subcontractors failed to sign a lien release. I'm not entirely sure how that happened, and we might not get to the bottom of it until Monday, when the bookkeeper gets back to the office, but I'm on it."

She stiffened. "I don't need your help."

"Maybe not, but you've got it anyway. And that has nothing to do with my father's interest in Rancho Esperanza. I told him it wasn't for sale and insisted that he back off and leave you alone."

She merely stared at him, her lips parted.

"I'm sorry for not coming clean when my memory began to return, but honey, I'm on your side. Not my father's."

She wanted to believe him. But...

"Ever since I passed the Texas bar, I've been working as the family attorney. And I've just begun to question my loyalty to my father."

"I don't understand."

"My dad has been purchasing ranches around here because he thinks the state might put a highway through the area. And if that's the case, they'll pay you for whatever stretch of property they might need. And there'll be a lot of businesses springing up, making some properties near Fairborn a lot more valuable than people think. But I know you like the ranch the way it is."

It all made sense. And she wanted to believe him, to trust him. But she didn't want to make another mistake by pinning her hopes and dreams on someone unworthy of her love.

"I'll admit," Clay said, "that my father sent me to Colorado to meet with you and to convince you to sell. But from the moment I saw you, all bets were off. Not only were you far more attractive than I'd been told but you were honest, genuine and—" He paused.

"And what?"

"Damn, Alana. I've never met anyone like you. And before the night was over, I realized that I didn't care whether you sold the ranch or not."

"And now?"

"I'm even more convinced that Rancho Esperanza belongs to the McGee family—and that it's rightfully yours."

God, how she longed to believe him.

He reached out and, using his knuckles, stroked her cheek. "When you suggested that we make love, my conscience rose up. I wanted to say something then and there, but I was so caught up in the moment, so swayed by you, that I went along with the idea. I promised myself that I'd tell you who I was in the morning."

"And then I left. While it was still dark."

He nodded. "When I woke up and found you gone, I felt an emptiness that left me stunned. And for the first time, I was at a complete loss as to what to do."

"So you waited to find me for four months?"

"Yes, but for what it's worth, your rejection really stung. More than anything I think I'd ever experienced."

She knew how that felt. Seeing him and his father in the yard yesterday, hearing them talk, realizing that they'd been plotting against her... or, at least, believing they were.

"Alana, I've been trying to fit in and be accepted by my father and half brothers for so damned long that I made up my mind I wasn't going to chase after you. I chalked up that evening to a one-night stand—as memorable as it was. And, believe it or not, I encouraged my father to focus on buying another Montana ranch, although he was dead set on having yours."

That fit, she supposed. And while she might be too naive, too stupid when it came to him, she wanted to believe him. Needed to believe him.

"I'm sorry," he said. "I hope you'll forgive me."

She didn't have to think about that very long. The sincerity in his eyes reached deep into her heart and soul. "I forgive you."

A slow smile stretched across his face. "I love you, Alana. And I want to be a part of our baby's life. I want to live with you here. On the ranch. But whether you desire a romantic relationship with me or not, know that my loyalty belongs only to you and to our son or daughter. You two are the only family I hope to be a part of."

She not only believed him, she saw the love in his eyes, felt it deep in her own heart, and she was lost. "I love you, too, Clay. I think I fell for you the moment you asked if you could sit at my table. And I've only come to love you more each day."

"You have no idea how badly I've wanted to hear you say that." Then he took her in his arms and kissed her, sweetly and soundly.

When the kiss ended, he placed his hand along her cheek and gazed into her eyes. "I'm taking you out to dinner tonight to celebrate."

"I have a better idea." She reached up, took his hand from her face, and just as she'd done the night they met, she led him down the hall and to her bedroom.

* * *

"I like the way you celebrate," Clay said, as he walked with Alana to her room.

"I thought you might." She tossed him a happy smile.

"But I still want to take you to dinner tonight," he said. "Someplace special."

"All right, but I'm not hungry right now."

"I am. Hungry for you."

As she began unbuttoning the front of her pale green dress, she kept her eyes peeled on him, watching him as carefully as he was watching her.

Damn, she was beautiful. And sexy. He was itching to touch her, to kiss her, to make love with her again. Over the past few days, he'd had a lot of memories come to mind, but none of them were as real or as memorable as the sight of sweet Alana wearing only a white lace bra and matching panties. This vision would be branded in his brain and in his heart for as long as he lived. "You take my breath away, honey."

She placed a hand on her baby bump, as if covering it from his view. Did she think it might be a turnoff? No way. It made her even more appealing.

He placed his hand over hers, where it rested over their child. "Don't hide your pregnancy.

Not from me. I like seeing you that way—and knowing I took part in creating our baby."

A flood of emotion swelled in her eyes—appreciation was one. And love was another. But passion burned bright.

The heat rushing through his veins damn near set the room ablaze, and he couldn't wait to celebrate what they were feeling for each other.

He removed his shirt and tossed it aside. Then, after shedding his boots, pants and boxer briefs, he kissed her again, taking it tantalizingly slow and easy, savoring the taste of her, the feel of her in his arms, the warmth of her touch.

He slid his hands along the curve of her back and down the slope of her hips.

She leaned into him, against his growing erection, and a surge of desire shot clear through him. When she drew her mouth from his, he felt an instant loss. But as she began to remove her bra, freeing two beautiful breasts, his blood began to pound a primal beat.

Once she removed her panties and had bared herself to him, she kissed him again. Her breasts pressed against his chest, skin to skin, heart to heart.

He continued to stroke her soft, silky flesh, to caress her curves. When he reached her breast, he brushed his thumb across a taut nipple. Her breath caught, and a liquid flame shot through his bloodstream. He continued to fondle her breasts, first one, then the other until he couldn't stand to prolong the foreplay any longer.

As if reading his mind, she slid out of his arms, climbed onto the bed and stretched out on top of the comforter. Then she opened her arms, silently inviting him to join her.

She didn't have to ask him twice. As he lay beside her, he kissed her again, taking up where they'd left off. Tasting, touching, stroking until he thought he might explode.

He hovered over her and searched her passion-glazed eyes. "Are you ready?"

"More than ready, Clay." She opened for him, reached for his erection and guided him…home.

He entered her, and she arched up to meet each of his thrusts. A climax built until the world stood still and they came together in a sexual explosion that turned him inside out—and every which way but loose.

He'd had other lovers before, but he'd never experienced anything like this. Anyone like her.

As they rested in an amazing afterglow, Clay turned to the side. They faced each other. Neither of them spoke. They just lay there, amazed at what they'd shared and the future that awaited them.

He reached out and touched the soft spot at the bottom of her throat. His fingers trailed along her chest, between her breasts and lower, to the growing bulge where their baby grew.

"Would it be okay if I went with you to your next doctor's appointment?" he asked.

"I'd love that. I'm glad you want to be involved."

He did, but it was even more than that. "I need to make sure you're healthy, that the baby is healthy. And I'd like to meet the doctor." He went on to share how his mother had lost a baby and how he didn't want anything to happen to her or to their child.

"Just a heads-up," he said. "I'm probably going to be worried the entire time."

"I'm glad you're concerned about us, but I don't want you to worry. I have a good doctor. She's one of the best in the area. According to her, the ultrasound looked fine, the baby's growing. So things are moving along as expected."

"That's good to know." He brushed a strand of hair from her brow. "I've been thinking about something else, too."

"What's that?"

"I'd like to help you make a go of the ranch. But I'd also like to take the Montana bar exam. I want to practice law in Fairborn. I might only work part-time, but I want to offer my services to people who need legal aid but can't afford it."

"That's very cool. I'd like that. We can rebuild

the ranch together. And you can help others rebuild their lives."

That's the way he saw it, too. He'd found his soul mate. The woman who'd be his best friend, his life's partner and his lover.

Forever and always.

Epilogue

It was a warm, bright August afternoon—but what made the day even more special is that Clay and Alana would be married in less than twenty-four hours. They'd chosen to have an outdoor wedding at Rancho Esperanza, and Clay couldn't think of a better place to recite their vows in front of their family and friends.

He'd just walked away from the copse of weeping willows down by the pond, where Alana's friend Marissa was instructing the party-rental guys where to set up the white gazebo and the chairs. Marissa was the one who'd suggested that Alana host weddings on the ranch, so she was eager to show them all what she had in mind.

She'd be here early tomorrow morning, too, and would be telling the florist how she wanted the flowers to adorn the gazebo. She'd be meeting with the baker, as well.

Clay had no more than reached the front yard when a white Cadillac Escalade pulled up and parked.

His steps slowed as he watched his father get out of the SUV. He was dressed, as usual, in his finest Western wear and carried the same high-end satchel he always took to business meetings.

Needless to say, his dad had been surprised to learn that Clay was getting married, and even more so to find out that Alana was pregnant with his first grandson. But those were only two of the many surprises Adam Hastings had received recently. The first was the news that Clay wouldn't be returning to Texas and the family would need another attorney. The second, and maybe most disconcerting, was that the proposed plan to build a state highway in this area had been postponed indefinitely. As luck would have it, the governor uncovered a couple of corrupt supervisors in the state transportation department, one of whom was his father's old college roommate.

"You're a day early," Clay told his dad. "The wedding's tomorrow."

"Yes, I know. But I thought I'd come by and

bring you a wedding gift so I can give it to you in private."

"Should I call Alana outside?" Clay asked. "Or would you rather go in the house?"

"Let's go inside. I've got something for the baby, too."

Once he'd learned that he was going to be a grandfather, Adam Hastings seemed to have softened. Or maybe he'd decided to turn over a new leaf after he'd barely escaped being linked to his buddy, the corrupt supervisor. Either way, he'd apologized to Alana for being so…forceful. And he promised to be more thoughtful in the future. Somehow, Clay wasn't so sure it was in his nature, since he did tend to lean more toward being what Alana had considered a pompous jerk. But Adam Hastings didn't apologize often, and he'd seemed to mean it.

Clay led him to the house. "I'm not sure what your plans are, Dad, but you're welcome to stay with us."

"I don't want to put you out, Clay. You two have probably got a lot going on today and tomorrow."

"True. But the offer stands." Clay opened the door. "Honey, my dad's here. And he'd like to talk to us."

Alana came out of the kitchen wearing a pair of black yoga pants and a lime green top that molded to her belly. Her baby bump seemed to have doubled in size this past month, a sign that everything was going well, just as the obstetrician assured Clay at each of the checkups he'd attended.

"Hi, Mr. Hastings." Alana greeted his father with a warm smile and a forgiving heart. "Can I get you a cup of coffee? I also have some blueberry muffins."

"Maybe later," his old man said, as he took a seat in the easy chair. "But I'd really like it if you'd consider calling me Dad, or even Adam, if you prefer. When I hear Mr. Hastings, I look around for my own father."

"All right," Alana said, "…Dad."

Clay was a bit surprised at his father's easy acceptance of Alana, but if there was one thing his father admired, it was a person who couldn't be bought—even if his dad was the one waving the cash in front of them like a carrot.

"By the way," his father said, as he turned his attention to Clay, "did they ever find those guys who assaulted you and robbed you blind?"

"As a matter of fact, the sheriff, Brandon Dodd, got a description of the men from Carlene Tipton, who owns the market. And he made an arrest last week."

"Good. Glad to hear it."

As Alana and Clay sat next to each other on

the sofa, Dad reached into his briefcase, pulled out a paper and handed it to them. "First of all, this is for you."

"What is it?" Clay asked.

"The deed to the ranch I bought a couple of months ago. I quitclaimed it to you and Alana. It's the ranch I bought from Olivia McGee."

"Wow," Alana said. "I don't know what to say. Thank you, Mr. Hastings. Oops. Sorry. I mean, Dad. I just didn't expect something so...huge. And so valuable."

"Seems only fair that you end up with that woman's property, especially after she tried to take yours away from you."

The man had a point. Olivia had cut a sweet deal when she'd sold her property, and she'd hoped to score big again when she'd contested Jack's will in an attempt to take possession of Rancho Esperanza. But that hadn't worked out in her favor.

"Besides," his old man added, "you wanted to be a rancher, Clay. So now you have room to double the spread."

Clay reached over and took Alana's hand, giving it an affectionate squeeze and joining them together as a team. "Thanks, Dad. We appreciate that."

"I've also started a college fund for the baby at Fairborn Savings and Trust," Dad added. "It's never too early to think about higher education. Who knows, he might want to go to law school."

As far as Clay was concerned, his son could be anything he wanted to be, follow any path he chose. All he wanted was for the boy to be healthy and to grow up to be an honest man of integrity.

"Now, then," his father said. "I do believe I'm ready for that cup of coffee. And I'll top it off with a muffin."

As Alana and Clay got to their feet, Clay slipped his arms around her and brushed a kiss on her brow.

"Thank you," he said.

Her head tilted slightly to the side. "For what?"

"For being so sweet, generous, kind and forgiving. I've never met anyone like you, and I can't wait to make you my wife."

Then he kissed her, long and deep, letting her know that he'd always have her back.

Today. Tomorrow. And always.

* * * * *

Look for Marissa's story,
the next installment in
USA TODAY *bestselling author Judy Duarte's*
new miniseries Rancho Esperanza
On sale June 2021
Available wherever Harlequin books
and ebooks are sold.

COMING NEXT MONTH FROM

H HARLEQUIN
SPECIAL EDITION

Available March 30, 2021

#2827 RUNAWAY GROOM
The Fortunes of Texas: The Hotel Fortune • by Lynne Marshall

When Mark Mendoza discovers his fiancée cheating on him on their wedding day, he hightails it out of town. Megan Fortune is there to pick up the pieces—and to act as his faux girlfriend when his ex shows up. Mark swears he will never get involved again. Megan doesn't want to be a "rebound" fling. But they find each other irresistible. What's a fake couple to do?

#2828 A NEW FOUNDATION
Bainbridge House • by Rochelle Alers

While restoring a hotel with his adoptive siblings, engineer Taylor Williamson hires architectural historian Sonja Rios-Martin. Neither of them ever thought they'd mix business with pleasure, but when their relationship runs into both of their pasts, they'll have to figure out if this passion is worth fighting for.

#2829 WYOMING MATCHMAKER
Dawson Family Ranch • by Melissa Senate

Divorced real estate agent Danica Dunbar still isn't ready for marriage and motherhood. When she has to care for her infant niece, Ford Dawson, the sexy detective who wants to settle down, is a little too helpful. Will this matchmaker pawn him off on someone else? Or is she about to make a match of her own?

#2830 THE RANCHER'S PROMISE
Match Made in Haven • by Brenda Harlen

Mitchell Gilmore was best man at Lindsay Delgado's wedding, "uncle" to her children and, when Lindsay is tragically widowed, a consoling shoulder. Until one electric kiss changes everything. Now Mitchell is determined to move from lifelong friendship to forever family. It's a risky proposition, but maybe Lindsay will finally make good on her promise.

#2831 THE TROUBLE WITH PICKET FENCES
Lovestruck, Vermont • by Teri Wilson

A pregnant former beauty queen and a veteran fire captain at the end of his rope realize it's never too late to build a family and that life, love and lemonade are sweeter when you let down your guard and open your heart to fate's most unexpected twists and turns.

#2832 THEIR SECOND-CHANCE BABY
The Parent Portal • by Tara Taylor Quinn

Annie Morgan needs her ex-husband's help—specifically, she needs him to sign over his rights to the embryos they had frozen prior to their divorce. But when she ends up pregnant—with twins—it becomes very clear their old feelings never left. Will their previous problems wreck their relationship once again?

YOU CAN FIND MORE INFORMATION ON UPCOMING HARLEQUIN TITLES,
FREE EXCERPTS AND MORE AT HARLEQUIN.COM.

HSECNM0321

*Mitchell Gilmore and Lindsay Delgado had been best
friends for as long as they could remember. He was
best man at her wedding, "uncle" to her children
and, when Lindsay is tragically widowed, a consoling
shoulder. Until one electric kiss changes everything.
Now Mitchell is determined to move from lifelong
friendship to forever family—if Lindsay can see that
he's ready to be a family man...*

Read on for a sneak peek at
The Rancher's Promise
*by Brenda Harlen,
the new book in her Match Made in Haven series!*

"Do you want coffee?" Lindsay asked.

"No, thanks."

"So...how was your date?"

Considering that it was over before nine o'clock,
she was surprised when Mitchell said, "Actually, it was
great. It turns out that Karli's not just beautiful but smart
and witty and fun. We had a great dinner and interesting
conversation."

She didn't particularly want to hear all the details, but
she'd been the one to insist they remain firmly within the
friend zone and, as a friend, it was her duty to listen.

"That is great," she said. Lied. "I'm happy for you." Another lie. "But I have to wonder, if she's so great… why are you here?"

"Because she's not you," he said simply. "And I don't want anyone but you."

She might have resisted the words, but the intensity and sincerity of his gaze sent them arrowing straight to her heart. Still, she had to be smart. To think about what was at stake.

"I know you're afraid to risk our friendship, and I understand why. But there's so much more we could have together. So much more we could be to one another. Don't we deserve a chance to find out?"

Before Lindsay could respond to either his confession or his question, he was kissing her.

Don't miss
The Rancher's Promise *by Brenda Harlen,*
available April 2021 wherever
Harlequin Special Edition books and ebooks are sold.

Harlequin.com

Get 4 FREE REWARDS!

We'll send you 2 FREE Books plus 2 FREE Mystery Gifts.

Harlequin Special Edition books relate to finding comfort and strength in the support of loved ones and enjoying the journey no matter what life throws your way.

FREE
Value Over
$20

*Return to Mustang Creek, Wyoming, and
The Brides of Bliss County series to discover if a
handsome single father reluctant to fall in love again
can be the right husband for a woman who wants it all.*

Read on for a sneak peek at Bex and Tate's story in
The Marriage Season *from #1 New York Times
bestselling author Linda Lael Miller.*

Bex Stuart was like a fishing sorceress if there was such
a thing. Once the five of them had piled into the fishing
boat—a tight fit, with several seats shared—he set off.
They weighed anchor in the middle of the lake, and she
cast in the first line.

Instant hit. She raised her brows at him and handed the
pole to Ben. "Can you reel it in for me?"

If she hadn't already been the boys' favorite, she sure
was now.

The boys caught on quickly. Aunt Bex tossed out the
bait and let you land the fish.

They had a grand time, and Tate didn't even get to
dip a line in the water, he was so busy. There were some
skillet-worthy catches, too, so he put them on a stringer
and was glad he'd dug out his fillet knife.

By midmorning they'd caught their limit and he was
able to give Bex—and himself—a break, announcing

that they needed to head back to town for more ice. They could have lunch there, too, he said—an idea that was generally endorsed.

After he'd docked the boat and the boys raced up the steps, he had to ask her, "How the hell did you do that?"

Her eyes were warm with laughter. "I warned you."

"I'd call you a witch," he murmured, "but I think *bewitching* is more appropriate."

And then he caught her hand, pulled her toward him and kissed her.

His mouth was warm, gentle but insistent, and his hands were firm on her shoulders. Bex relaxed into the kiss despite being cold and more than a little damp from the mist. The shiver she felt wasn't related to the weather.

The kiss was good.

Too good.

She was the one to finally break away. A potentially combustible situation was getting more and more volatile with each passing second, and there was nothing they could do about it. Not on this trip, and not when they were back in Mustang Creek, either. He'd always have the boys. She had not only Josh but Tara, too, on her hands. Plus, she had a growing business, and he was building a house, starting his own business, as well…

It was just too complicated.

Don't miss
The Marriage Season *from #1 New York Times bestselling author Linda Lael Miller, available now wherever HQN books are sold!*

HQNBooks.com